D1323757

Praise for *Kim Jiyoung, Born 1982*

'I loved this novel. Kim Jiyoung's life is made to seem at once
totally commonplace and nightmarishly over-the-top. As you
read, you constantly feel that revolutionary, electric shift, between
commonplace and nightmarish. This kind of imaginative
work is so important and so powerful. I hope this book
sells a million more copies.'
Elif Batuman, author of *The Idiot*
(shortlisted for the Women's Prize)

'I imagine the million Korean copies of *Kim Jiyoung, Born 1982* as
a kind of membership card or printed creed – proof of a
collective experience too often demeaned.'
New York Review of Books

'*Kim Jiyoung, Born 1982* has much in common
with Han Kang's *The Vegetarian*.'
Los Angeles Review of Books

'Though she's a fictional character, Kim Jiyoung is a symbolic figure
in Korea. It seems her status will be even more elevated as novel
Kim Jiyoung, Born 1982 recently became a million-copy bestseller.'
Korea Herald

'Not only a riveting read, but a mirror to society that is daring
enough to portray us as faceless as we truly are.'
Korean Literature Now

'It has touched the hearts of readers of diverse backgrounds across
Korea for its subtleness. Rather than depicting extreme situations for
the sake of the plot, the book calmly describes common experiences
that happen in the everyday lives of Korean women – things that
have always been there, but have never been
thought of as problematic until recently.'
Korea JoongAng Daily

KIM JIYOUNG, BORN 1982

Palsip Yi Nyeon Saeng Kim Jiyeong

CHO NAM-JOO

TRANSLATED BY JAMIE CHANG

SCRIBNER

LONDON NEW YORK SYDNEY TORONTO NEW DELHI

First published in Great Britain by Scribner,
an imprint of Simon & Schuster UK Ltd, 2020
A CBS COMPANY

Originally published in Korea by Minumsa Publishing Co., Ltd., Seoul, 2016

Copyright © *Palsip Yi Nyeon Saeng Kim Jiyeong* by Cho Nam-joo, 2016
Translation © Jamie Chang, 2018

SCRIBNER and design are registered trademarks of The Gale Group, Inc.,
used under licence by Simon & Schuster Inc.

The right of Cho Nam-joo to be identified as the author of
this work has been asserted in accordance with the
Copyright, Designs and Patents Act, 1988.

1 3 5 7 9 10 8 6 4 2

Simon & Schuster UK Ltd
1st Floor
222 Gray's Inn Road
London WC1X 8HB

www.simonandschuster.co.uk
www.simonandschuster.com.au
www.simonandschuster.co.in

Simon & Schuster Australia, Sydney
Simon & Schuster India, New Delhi

This book is a work of fiction. Names, characters, places
and incidents are either a product of the author's imagination or
are used fictitiously. Any resemblance to actual people living or
dead, events or locales is entirely coincidental.

A CIP catalogue record for this book
is available from the British Library

Trade Paperback ISBN: 978-1-4711-8428-4
eBook ISBN: 978-1-4711-8429-1

Typeset in Palatino by M Rules
Printed and bound by CPI Group (UK) Ltd, Croydon CR0 4YY

CONTENTS

Autumn, 2015

Kim Jiyoung is thirty-three years old, or thirty-four in Korean age. She got married three years ago and had a daughter last year. She rents a small apartment on the outskirts of Seoul with her husband Jung Daehyun, thirty-six, and daughter Jung Jiwon. Daehyun works at a mid-size IT company, and Jiyoung used to work at a small marketing agency, which she left a few weeks before her due date. Daehyun usually comes home from work around midnight and goes into the office at least once on weekends. Daehyun's parents live in Busan, and Jiyoung's parents run a restaurant, making Jiyoung her daughter's sole carer. Just after Jiwon turned one in the summer, she started daycare as a half-day infant. She spends her mornings at a converted ground-floor apartment daycare centre in the same apartment complex where she lives.

Jiyoung's abnormal behaviour was first detected on 8 September. Daehyun remembers the exact date because it was the morning of *baengno* ('white dew'), the first night of autumn when the temperature drops below dew point. Daehyun was having toast and milk for breakfast when Jiyoung suddenly went to the veranda and opened the window. It was quite sunny out, but the cold air rushed in as soon as the window was opened and reached the kitchen table where Daehyun was sitting.

Jiyoung returned to the table with her shoulders hunched and, as she sat down, said, 'I knew there was a little nip in the air these past few mornings, and today's *baengno*! White morning dew on fields of *gooold*, on *baengno* when the nights grow *cooold*.'

Daehyun laughed at his wife, who was talking like a much older woman.

'What's up with you? You sound like your mum.'

'Take a light jacket with you, Jung *seoba-ahng*. There's a chill in the mornings and evenings.'

Even then, he thought she was just joking around. Her imitation of her mother was flawless, down to her signature right-eye wink when she was asking for a favour, and the elongated last syllable of 'Jung *seobang*'. He had found her staring off into space or crying over sad songs, but Daehyun figured she was just exhausted from taking care of the baby. She was basically a cheerful person, full of laughter, who often made Daehyun laugh by doing impressions of celebrities. So Daehyun shrugged off Jiyoung's imitation of her mother, gave her a hug and went to work.

When Daehyun came back from work that night, she was sleeping next to their daughter. Both were sucking their thumbs, looking cute but absurd. Gazing at the two side by side, he tugged at his wife's arm to pull her thumb out of her mouth. Jiyoung's tongue stuck out a little and she smacked her lips, just like a baby, and then settled back into sleep.

A few days later, Jiyoung said that she was Cha Seungyeon, a college friend who had died a year before. Seungyeon and Daehyun started college the same year and Jiyoung had been their junior by three years. All three were members of the same university hiking club. However, Jiyoung and Daehyun didn't know each other in college. Daehyun wanted to go on to graduate school, but had to give up due to family circumstances. After he completed his third year of university, he took time off to belatedly fulfil his military service, after which he returned to his home in Busan to work part-time for a year. Jiyoung had entered college and was an active hiking club member during his time away.

Seungyeon had always been good to her fellow female club members, on top of which she and Jiyoung had something in common: they didn't actually enjoy hiking. They became friends and kept in touch and met up frequently even after Seungyeon graduated. In fact, Seungyeon's wedding reception was the very occasion on which Daehyun and Jiyoung met for the first time. Seungyeon died giving birth to her second child due to an amniotic fluid embolism. Jiyoung was suffering from postpartum depression when she heard about Seungyeon's death, and the shocking news on top of everything else made it hard for her to handle everyday tasks.

After their daughter had gone to sleep, the couple relaxed and drank some beers, something they hadn't done in a while. When Jiyoung had almost finished a can of beer, she tapped her husband on the shoulder and abruptly said, 'Hey, Jiyoung is having a hard time. Raising a toddler is emotionally draining. You should tell her every chance you get: *You're doing great! You're working so hard! I appreciate you!*'

'Are you astral-projecting, hon? Fine, fine. Yes, you're doing great, Kim Jiyoung. I know that you're going through a tough time. I appreciate you and I love you.' Daehyun lovingly pinched her cheek, but she swatted his hand away, irritated.

4

'You still see me as the lovestruck twenty-year-old Cha Seungyeon? Who shook like a leaf in the middle of summer confessing her feelings?'

Daehyun's heart stopped. That was almost twenty years ago. In the middle of the day in the middle of summer, in the middle of the university athletics field, yards away from the tiniest spot of shade. The blazing sun was beating down on the two of them. He couldn't remember how they ended up there, but he'd run into Seungyeon who suddenly said she liked him. She liked him, she had feelings for him, she had said, sweat pouring, lips trembling, stammering. Daehyun gave her an apologetic look, and she instantly folded.

'Oh, you don't feel the same. Got it. Forget what I said. Forget this whole thing happened. I'll treat you the same as before, like nothing happened.'

And with that, she trotted across the field and disappeared. She really did treat him the same as before, as if nothing had happened and so casually that Daehyun wondered if the whole thing had been a sun exposure-induced hallucination. He never thought about it again. And here was his own wife bringing it back – a scene from a sunny afternoon almost twenty years ago that only two people in the world knew about.

'Jiyoung,' was all Daehyun could say. He might have mumbled her name three more times.

'Hah dude, stop calling me by her name. I get it, I know – you're a model husband!'

Hah dude, Cha Seungyeon used to say over and over when she was drunk. His hair stood on end and he felt something like electric currents spreading over his scalp. Pretending to be unfazed, he kept telling her to stop kidding around. Jiyoung, leaving her empty can on the table, went to the bedroom and lay down next to her daughter without brushing her teeth. She immediately fell fast asleep. Daehyun got himself another beer and knocked it back. Was this some kind of joke? Was she drunk? Was she possessed by a spirit or something, like those people on TV?

The next morning, Jiyoung came out of the bedroom massaging her temples. She didn't seem to remember what had happened the night before. On the one hand, he was relieved to think she had simply been drunk, but on the other hand, that was one spooky drinking habit. He also found it hard to believe that she had actually been drunk and blacked out. She'd only had one can of beer.

Her odd behaviour continued sporadically. She'd send him a text message riddled with cute emoticons she never normally used, or make dishes like ox-bone soup or glass noodles that she neither enjoyed nor was good at. Jiyoung was starting to feel like a stranger to Daehyun. After all this time – the stories they shared, as countless as rain-drops, the caresses as soft and gentle as snowflakes, and the beautiful daughter who took after them both – his wife of three years, whom he married after two years of passionate romance, felt like someone else.

Then came the *Chuseok* harvest holidays. They were vis-iting Daehyun's parents down in Busan. Daehyun took Friday off, and the three of them left home at seven in the morning and arrived in Busan five hours later. They had lunch with Daehyun's parents immediately after they arrived, and Daehyun, tired from the long drive, took a nap. Daehyun and Jiyoung used to take turns at the wheel on long drives, but ever since their daughter was born, Daehyun did all the driving. The baby fussed, whined and cried every time they put her in the car seat, and Jiyoung was better at keeping her occupied and happy by playing with her and giving her snacks.

Jiyoung did the dishes after lunch, took a coffee break and went to the market with her mother-in-law to shop for *Chuseok* food. They spent the afternoon boiling the ox bone, marinating ribs, prepping and blanching the vege-tables to season some and freeze the rest for later, washing and preparing seafood for the next day's pancakes and fritters, making, eating and clearing dinner.

The next day, Jiyoung and Daehyun's mother flipped pancakes, fried fritters, stewed ribs and sculpted rice cakes. The family ate freshly made holiday dishes and enjoyed themselves. Their daughter, Jiwon, felt right at home in the arms and laps of her grandparents, who showered the affectionate child with love.

The day after that was *Chuseok*. Daehyun's older cousin was in charge of the ancestral rites, so Daehyun's family didn't have much to do on the day itself. Everyone slept in, had a simple breakfast of food made the day before, finished the dishes, and Suhyun, Daehyun's younger sister, arrived with her family. Two years younger than Daehyun and a year older than Jiyoung, Suhyun lived in Busan with her husband and two sons, and her in-laws lived in Busan as well. Her father-in-law being the eldest of his male siblings, Suhyun was under a great deal of pressure during the holidays to make food for the ancestral rites and wait on the guests. Suhyun passed out as soon as she arrived. Jiyoung and Daehyun's mother made soup from the ox-bone broth, cooked a fresh batch of rice, grilled fish and seasoned vegetables for lunch.

After lunch was cleared, Suhyun brought out a big bag of gifts for Jiwon: dresses of all colours, a tutu, hair slides, lace socks and so on. Suhyun put slides in Jiwon's hair and socks on her feet, admiring the baby girl. *I wish I had a daughter. Daughters are the best.* In the meantime, Jiyoung brought out plates of apple and pear slices, but everyone was so full from lunch they barely touched them. When she brought out rice cakes, Suhyun took a piece.

'Mum, did you make this at home?'

'Of course I did.'

'Mum, how many times do I have to tell you? Don't make food at home! I was going to mention this before, but don't make ox-bone broth, either. Buy the pancakes at the market, and get the rice cakes from the shop. Why do you make so much food when we don't even hold ancestral rites here? You're too old for this, and it's hard on Jiyoung.'

Disappointment flashed across the mother's face. 'It isn't work when you're feeding your own family. The point of the holidays is to get together, make and eat food together.' She turned to Jiyoung and put her on the spot: 'Was it too much for you?'

At this, Jiyoung's expression softened, her cheeks flushed into a gentle pink, and a warm smile emerged in her eyes. Daehyun was nervous. Jiyoung responded before he could change the subject or get her out of there. 'Oh, Mrs Jung. To tell you the truth, my poor Jiyoung gets sick from exhaustion every holiday!'

Time stood still in the room. It was as if they suddenly found themselves sitting atop a great iceberg. Suhyun finally broke the silence by letting out a long, frosty sigh that dissolved in the air.

'Ji, Jiwon needs a nappy change, no?'

Daehyun belatedly grabbed Jiyoung by the hand, but she swatted him off.

'Jung *seoba-ahng*! You're to blame, too! You spend all your holidays in Busan and drop by our place just for a quick bite. This year, try to come earlier,' she said, winking her right eye.

Right at that moment, Suhyun's six-year-old son fell off the sofa while playing with his little brother. He began to howl in pain, but no one had the mind to tend to him. He took a look at the adults sitting there, mouths agape, and stopped crying on his own.

'What is this nonsense?' Daehyun's father thundered. 'Is this how you behave in front of your elders? Daehyun, Suhyun and everyone else in our family only get together a few times a year. Is this really something to complain about – spending time with family?'

'Father, that's not what she's saying,' Daehyun tried to explain, but he didn't know how to start.

'Mr Jung, with all due respect, I must say my piece,' Jiyoung said in a cool tone, pushing Daehyun aside. 'As you know, the holidays are a time for families to gather. But they're not just for your family. They're for my family, too. Everyone's so busy nowadays and it's hard for my children to get together, too, if not for the holidays. You should at least let our daughter come home when your daughter comes to visit you.'

In the end, Daehyun had to cup his hand over Jiyoung's mouth and drag her out.

'She's not well, Father. You've got to believe me, Mum, Father. Suhyun, too. She hasn't been well lately. I'll explain everything later.'

Daehyun got his wife and daughter in the car so fast that they didn't even have time to button their coats. Once in the car himself, Daehyun pressed his head against the steering wheel, overwhelmed. Meanwhile, Jiyoung sang to their daughter as if nothing had happened. His parents didn't even come out to say goodbye. Instead, Suhyun appeared carrying her brother's bags and put them in the trunk.

'Jiyoung's right,' said Suhyun. 'We've been inconsiderate. Don't fight or argue about it. Don't get mad. Just say that you're grateful and you're sorry. Got it?'

'I'm off now. Talk to Father for me.'

Daehyun wasn't angry – he was baffled, sad and scared.

Daehyun visited the psychiatrist alone to discuss Jiyoung's symptoms and treatment options. He told his wife, who didn't seem to be aware of her condition, that he had booked a therapy session for her since she hadn't been sleeping well and seemed stressed. Jiyoung thanked him, saying that she had indeed been feeling blue and enervated, and that she suspected maternity blues.

CHILDHOOD, 1982–1994

Kim Jiyoung was born on 1 April 1982 at an obstetrics clinic in Seoul. She measured 50cm and weighed 2.9kg. At the time of her birth, her father was a civil servant and her mother a housewife. Jiyoung's elder sister had been born two years earlier, and a brother was born five years later. In a roughly 35-square-metre house with two bedrooms, one dining and living room, and one bathroom, Jiyoung lived with her grandmother, parents and two siblings.

Jiyoung's earliest childhood memory is of sneaking her brother's formula. She must have been six or seven then. It was just formula, but it was so tasty she would sit by her mother when she was making it for her brother, lick her finger, and pick up the little bits that spilled on the floor. Her mother would sometimes lean Jiyoung's head back, tell her to open wide, and pour a spoonful of that rich, sweet, nutty powder in her mouth. The formula would mix with her saliva, melt into a sticky mass, then turn soft as caramel, before sliding down the back of her throat and leaving a strange feeling in her mouth that wasn't quite dry or bitter.

Koh Boonsoon, Jiyoung's grandmother who lived with them, detested the very idea of Jiyoung eating her brother's formula. If her grandmother ever caught her getting a spoonful of it, she would smack her on the back so hard powder exploded from her mouth and nose. Kim Eunyoung, Jiyoung's big sister, never ate formula after the one time she was admonished by their grandmother.

'You don't like formula?'

'I do.'

'So why don't you eat it?'

'It stinks.'

'What?'

'I don't want their stinking formula. No way.'

Jiyoung couldn't understand what she meant by that, but she understood how she felt. Their grandmother wasn't scolding them just because they were too old for formula or because she was worried there wouldn't be enough formula for the baby. The combination of her tone, expression, angle of head tilt, position of shoulders and her breathing sent them a message that was hard to summarise in one sentence, but, if Jiyoung tried anyway, it went something like this: *How dare you try to take something that belongs to my precious grandson!* Her grandson and his things were valuable and to be cherished; she wasn't going to let just anybody touch them, and Jiyoung ranked below this 'anybody'. Eunyoung probably had the same impression.

It was a given that fresh rice hot out of the cooker was served in the order of father, brother and grandmother, and that perfect pieces of tofu, dumplings and patties were the brother's while the girls ate the ones that fell apart. The brother had chopsticks, socks, long underwear, and school and lunch bags that matched, while the girls made do with whatever was available. If there were two umbrellas, the girls shared. If there were two blankets, the girls shared. If there were two treats, the girls shared. It didn't occur to the child Jiyoung that her brother was receiving special treatment, and so she wasn't even jealous. That's how it had always been. There were times when she had an inkling of a situation not being fair, but she was accustomed to rationalising things by telling herself that she was being a generous older sibling and that she shared with her sister because they were both girls. Jiyoung's mother would praise the girls for taking good care of their brother and not competing for her love. Jiyoung thought it must be the big age gap. The more their mother praised, the more impossible it became for Jiyoung to complain.

Kim Jiyoung's father was the third of four brothers. The eldest died in a car accident before he married, and the second brother emigrated to the United States early on and settled down. The youngest brother and Jiyoung's father had a big fight over inheritance and looking after their mother that led to a falling-out.

The four brothers were born and raised at a time when mere survival was a struggle. As people died, young and old, of war, disease and starvation, Koh Boonsoon worked someone else's field, peddled someone else's wares, took care of domestic labour at someone else's home, and still managed to run her own home, fighting tooth and nail to raise the four boys. Her husband, a man with a fair complexion and soft hands, never worked a day in his life. Koh Boonsoon did not resent her husband for having neither the ability nor the will to provide for his family. She truly believed he was a decent husband to her for not sleeping around and not hitting her. Of the four sons she raised thus, Jiyoung's father was the only one to carry out his duties as a son in her old age. Unwanted by her ungrateful children, Koh Boonsoon rationalised this sad outcome with an incoherent logic: 'Still, I get to eat warm food my son made for me, and sleep under warm covers my son arranged for me because I had four sons. You have to have at least four sons.'

Oh Misook, her son's wife, was the one who cooked the warm food and laid out the warm covers for her, not her son, but Koh Boonsoon had a habit of saying so anyway. Easy-going considering the life she'd had, and relatively caring towards her daughter-in-law compared to other mothers-in-law of her generation, she would say from the bottom of her heart, for her daughter-in-law's sake, 'You should have a son. You must have a son. You must have at least two sons ...'

When Kim Eunyoung was born, Oh Misook held the infant in her arms and wept. 'I'm sorry, Mother,' she'd said, hanging her head.

Koh Boonsoon said warmly to her daughter-in-law, 'It's okay. The second will be a boy.'

When Kim Jiyoung was born, Oh Misook held the infant in her arms and wept. 'I'm sorry, little girl,' she'd said, hanging her head.

Koh Boonsoon repeated warmly to her daughter-in-law, 'It's okay. The third will be a boy.'

Oh Misook became pregnant with her third child less than a year after Jiyoung was born. One night, she dreamt that a tiger the size of a house came knocking down the front door and jumping into her lap. She was sure it was a boy. But the old lady obstetrician who delivered Eunyoung and Jiyoung scanned her lower abdomen several times with a grim look on her face and said cautiously, 'The baby is so, so . . . pretty. Like her sisters . . .'

Back at home, Oh Misook wept and wept and threw up everything she'd eaten that day, while Koh Boonsoon heard her daughter-in-law retching in the bathroom and sent her congratulations through the door.

'Your morning sickness is awful this time! You never got sick once when you were pregnant with Eunyoung and Jiyoung. This one must be different.'

Reluctant to leave the bathroom, Oh Misook locked herself in, to cry and throw up some more. Late that night, after the girls had gone to sleep, Oh Misook asked her husband, who was tossing and turning, 'What if . . . What if the baby is another girl? What would you do, Daddy?'

She was hoping for, *What do you mean, what would I do? Boy or girl, we'll raise it with love.* But there was no answer.

'Hmm?' she prodded. 'What would you do, Daddy?'

He rolled over to face the wall and said, 'Hush and go to sleep. Don't give the devil ideas.'

Oh Misook cried all night into her pillow, biting her lower lip so as not to make a sound. Morning came to find her pillow soaked and her lip so badly swollen that she couldn't stop herself from drooling.

This was a time when the government had implemented birth control policies called 'family planning' to keep population growth under control. Abortion due to medical problems had been legal for ten years at that point, and checking the sex of the foetus and aborting females was common practice, as if 'daughter' was a medical problem.[1] This went on throughout the 1980s, and in the early 1990s, the very height of the male-to-female ratio imbalance, when the ratio for the third child and beyond was over two-to-one.[2] Oh Misook went to the clinic by herself and 'erased' Jiyoung's younger sister. None of it was her fault, but all the responsibility fell on her, and no family was around to comfort her through her harrowing physical and emotional pain. The doctor held Oh Misook's hand as she howled like an animal that had lost its young to a beast and said, 'I'm sorry for your loss.' Thanks to the old lady doctor's words, Oh Misook was able to avoid losing her mind.

It was years before Oh Misook fell pregnant again, and the boy made it safely into this world. That boy is the brother five years younger than Jiyoung.

Being a civil servant, Jiyoung's father had a stable job and a steady income. But it was certainly a challenge for a family

---

1 Park Jaehyun, *Statistical Family*, (Mati Books, 2015), pp.57–58; 'Roots of Misogyny?', Cheon Gwanyul, September 2015, *Sisa In Magazine*.
2 *Sex Ratio at Birth by Birth Order*. Statistics Korea.

of six to live on the wages of a low-level government employee. As the three children grew, the two-bedroom house started to feel crowded, and Jiyoung's mother wanted to move to a bigger place where she could give the girls, who were sharing with their grandmother at the time, their own room.

Mother did not commute to a job like Father did, but was always doing odd jobs on the side that allowed her to make money while doing chores all on her own and looking after three children and an elderly mother-in-law. This was common among mothers in the neighbourhood who were more or less in the same situation. There was a boom in made-for-housewife jobs, all with the label *ajumma*, or middle-aged married woman: insurance *ajumma*, milk and Yakult *ajumma*, cosmetics *ajumma* and so on. Most companies outsourced their hiring, leaving the employees to their own devices if there were disputes or injuries on the job.[3] With three children to look after, Mother chose sideline work she could do from home. Taking out stitches, assembling cardboard boxes, folding envelopes, peeling garlic and rolling weather strips were just a few of the endless list of jobs available. Jiyoung helped her mother, usually with the clean-up afterwards or counting units.

---

3 Kim Sihyung, *Work Unrecorded*, (Samchang, 2016), pp. 21–29.

The trickiest job was rolling weather strips. Long, narrow pieces of spongy material, with film-protected adhesive on one side, would arrive at the house, and it was Mother's job to roll the strips up two at a time and put them in a small plastic wrapper. Mother held each weather strip lightly between her left thumb and index finger, as if to simply keep it in place, and rolled with the right hand. Pulling and rolling the weather strips, she often cut her finger on the paper film on the adhesive side. She wore two layers of work gloves, but her finger always bled anyway. The material took up a lot of space, the work produced a great deal of debris, and the fumes from the sponge and adhesive gave her a headache, but the pay was the best among all the odd jobs. Mother kept taking on more, and worked longer hours.

Father would often come home from work to find Mother still rolling weather strips. Jiyoung and Eunyoung, in elementary school at the time, sat in the living room with their mother, variously doing homework, goofing around and helping her, and their baby brother enjoyed himself ripping up pieces of sponge and wrapping plastic. On days when she had too much work, the family would push the pile of weather strips aside and have dinner next to it.

One day, Father came home from the office later than usual to find his young children still rolling around in weather strips, and complained for the first time: 'Do you really have to leave this smelly, dusty stuff around the children?'

Her busy hands and shoulders suddenly stopped. She crawled around, putting away the wrapped weather strips in boxes, and Father knelt down next to her to sweep sponge and pieces of paper into a large plastic bag.

'I wish I could give you an easier life. I'm sorry,' he said and let out a heavy sigh. A huge shadow seemed to balloon over him and fade away.

Mother lifted and stacked boxes bigger than herself in the living room, and swept the floor next to Father.

'You're not giving me a hard life, Daddy,' she said. 'We're working hard together to make it. So stop feeling sorry for yourself as if our home is your responsibility alone. No one is asking you to, and, frankly, you're not doing it on your own,' Mother retorted coldly, but she quit the weather strip job right away. The van driver who delivered the weather strips was sorry to hear it – she was the best and the fastest worker.

'It's just as well,' said the van driver. 'Your talents are too good to waste on weather strips. You should get into arts and crafts. I think you'll be good at it.'

She waved him off saying she was too old to learn new things. She was thirty-five at the time. The van driver's words seemed to have made an impression on Mother, who left young Eunyoung in charge of the even younger Jiyoung, and the youngest in the care of his grandmother, and enrolled on a course. It wasn't arts and crafts, but hairdressing. She didn't even bother with licences. 'You don't need a licence to cut hair,' she said. As soon as she picked up a few simple skills, how to cut and perm hair, she started making cheap house calls for children and the elderly around the neighbourhood.

Word spread. Mother was indeed talented, and had natural business savvy she was oblivious to. After their perms, old ladies got a simple makeover using Mother's eyeliner and lipstick, and she threw in a quick trim for the younger sibling or the mother after cutting a child's hair. She found out what product they used at the neighbourhood hair salon, and used something slightly more expensive on purpose.

She would read the label on the bottle to the old ladies, pointing to each word in the copy. 'See here? New. Irritation-free. Formula. With. Ginseng. Extract. I've never had a single piece of ginseng in my life, but I'm treating your hair with it!'

Mother saved every last bit of cash she made and didn't pay any tax on it. The neighbourhood hair salon lady did try to pull out a chunk of her hair for stealing her customers, but Mother was a local with a well-cultivated reputation – the customers took her side. The customer base was eventually divided up organically, and the salon and Mother were able to keep their businesses going without getting in each other's way.

Oh Misook, Kim Jiyoung's mother, is the fourth of five children, two boys, two girls and a boy, in that order. All five grew up and left home. Her family grew rice and did well for generations, but the world was changing. Traditionally an agricultural society, Korea was industrialising fast, and her family couldn't get by on crops alone. Her father sent his children to the cities like most parents from rural areas did in those days. But he didn't have the means to support all five of them through school or training that would lead to their respective career choices. In the city, rent and living costs were expensive, and tuition was even more difficult to afford.

Oh Misook finished elementary school and helped out around the house and in the paddies. She moved to Seoul the year she turned fifteen. Her sister, two years older than her, was working at a textile factory on Cheonggyecheon. Oh Misook got a job at the same factory and moved into a chicken coop dormitory the two sisters shared with two other girls. The factory girls were all about the same age, level of education, family background and so on. The young labourers worked without adequate sleep, rest or food, thinking that was what working entailed for everyone. The heat from the textile machines was enough to drive a person insane, and rolling up their uniform skirts, which were short to begin with, didn't help – sweat dripped from their elbows and down their thighs. Many had respiratory problems from the plumes of dust that sometimes obscured their vision. The unbelievably meagre wages from working day and night, popping caffeine pills and turning jaundiced, went towards sending male siblings to school. This was a time when people believed it was up to the sons to bring honour and prosperity to the family, and that the family's wealth and happiness hinged upon male success. The daughters gladly supported the male siblings.[4]

Oh Misook's eldest brother attended medical school at a national university outside of Seoul and worked at the university hospital at his alma mater for the rest of his career, and the second eldest brother was police chief by the time he retired. Oh Misook was proud of her upstanding, hardworking, smart elder brothers and found supporting them rewarding. When her older brothers, the ones she was so proud of she would often brag about them to her friends at the factory, began to earn a living, they put the youngest boy through school. He attended a

---

4 Park Jaehyun, *Statistical Family*, (Mati Books, 2015), p.61.

teacher training college in Seoul thanks to their support, and the eldest was praised for being the responsible first-born son who brought honour to the family through his own success and provided for his family. Oh Misook and her sister realised only then that their turn would not come; their loving family would not be giving them the chance and support to make something of themselves. The two sisters belatedly enrolled in the company-affiliated school. They worked days and studied nights to earn their middle-school diploma. Oh Misook studied for her high-school certificate on her own and received her diploma the same year her younger brother became a high-school teacher.

When Kim Jiyoung was in elementary school, her mother was reading a one-line comment her homeroom teacher had made on her journal assignment and said, 'I wanted to be a teacher, too.'

Jiyoung burst into laughter. She found the idea outrageous because she'd thought until then that mothers could only be mothers.

'It's true. In elementary, I got the best grades out of all five of us. I was better than your eldest uncle.'

'So why didn't you become a teacher?'

'I had to work to send my brothers to school. That's how it was with everyone. All women lived like that back then.'

'Why don't you become a teacher now?'

'Now I have to work to send you kids to school.' That's how it is with everyone. All mothers live like this these days.'

Her life choices, being Kim Jiyoung's mother – Oh Misook was regretting them. Jiyoung felt she was a rock, small but heavy and unyielding, holding down her mother's long skirt train. This made her sad. Her mother saw this and warmly swept back her daughter's unkempt hair.

———

Kim Jiyoung attended a very large elementary school that was twenty minutes away on foot along winding alleys. Each grade had between eleven and fifteen classes, fifty students to a class. Before Jiyoung entered, the school had been forced to split the lower grades into morning and afternoon classes to accommodate everyone.

Elementary school was Jiyoung's first social experience, as she did not attend kindergarten, and on the whole she did well. After an adjustment period, Eunyoung was put in charge of getting Jiyoung to school. Eunyoung checked the timetable each morning and packed her sister's books, notebooks and class announcements log, and filled her fairy princess pencil case with one eraser and four pencils that were not too sharp or too blunt. On days Jiyoung needed extra supplies, Eunyoung asked Mother for money and picked up the items at the stationery store by the school gate. Jiyoung walked to and from school without wandering off, stayed in her seat during class and did not wet herself. She wrote down the daily announcements in her class announcements log, and sometimes got 100 per cent on her dictation quizzes.

Her first obstacle in school life was the 'pranks of the boy desk-mate' that many schoolgirls experienced. To Jiyoung, it felt more like harassment or violence than pranks, and there was nothing she could do about it besides run crying to Mother and Eunyoung. They weren't much help. Eunyoung said boys were immature and that Jiyoung should just ignore him, and Mother chided Jiyoung for crying and complaining over a classmate who was just messing around because he wanted to play.

One day the desk-mate started to hit her. Sitting down, getting in line, picking up his schoolbag, he would hit her on the shoulder as if by accident. When he saw her coming down the hall he swerved to her side and knocked hard into her arm. He would borrow her eraser, pencil or ruler and not give it back. When she told him to give it back, he'd toss it across the room, or sit on it, or swear he never took it. He even got her in trouble in class for arguing over something he borrowed. When she stopped lending him her things, he moved on to making fun of the way she dressed, the words she misspoke, and hiding her schoolbag and shoe pouch in places that would take her forever to find.

One early summer day, Jiyoung had taken off her indoor shoes during class to cool her sweaty feet when the desk-mate suddenly scooted way down in his chair and kicked one of her shoes hard. The shoe went flying down the aisle all the way to the podium at the front of the class. The children instantly burst out laughing, and the teacher turned red with indignation.

'Whose shoe is it?' the teacher shouted, banging her fists on the podium.

Jiyoung couldn't speak up. She was scared, and although it was her shoe, she was hoping her desk-mate who kicked it would speak up first. But he must have been scared, too, as he kept his head down.

'Well? Speak up! Or should I check everyone's shoes?'

Jiyoung jabbed the desk-mate with her elbow and whispered, 'You did it.' He bowed his head even lower and said, 'It's not *my* shoe.' The teacher slammed the podium once again, and Jiyoung had to raise her hand. She was called out to the podium and scolded in front of the whole class. She was a cowardly liar for not answering the first time she asked whose shoe it was, and a thief who stole her classmates' valuable class time. Jiyoung was blubbing so hard, tears and snot everywhere, she couldn't say a word in her defence. Just then, someone said very quietly,

'It wasn't Jiyoung.' It was the girl who sat all the way at the back across the aisle.

'It's Jiyoung's shoe, but she didn't kick it. I saw.'

The confused teacher asked the girl, 'What do you mean? Then who did it?'

The girl seemed afraid to rat on him, but managed to quietly stare at the back of his head. The teacher and the class all looked at Jiyoung's desk-mate, and he finally confessed to the crime. The teacher scolded the desk-mate twice as loudly and for twice as long as she scolded Jiyoung. She was also twice as red in the face.

'You've been picking on Jiyoung, haven't you? You think I haven't been watching you? When you go home tonight, you're going to write down everything you ever did to harass her and bring it tomorrow. I know everything, so don't you even think about leaving things out. Write with your mother, and get her to sign it!'

The desk-mate went home dejected, sighing, 'Mum's gonna kill me.' The teacher told Jiyoung to stay behind after school.

Jiyoung was nervous as she expected another telling-off, but, much to her surprise, the teacher sat down in front of her and apologised. She was sorry she reprimanded Jiyoung without getting to the bottom of it, she thought the shoe belonged to the person who kicked it, it was unwise of her to make assumptions, and that she would be more attentive in the future. Jiyoung's heart melted at the teacher's words of apology and her promise to keep these misunderstandings from happening again. When the teacher asked if there was anything Jiyoung wanted to say, Jiyoung replied through a fit of tears and hiccups, 'Please – *hic hic* – assign me – *hic hic* – a new desk-mate. I don't – *hic hic* – ever, ever want to be – *hic hic* – desk-mates with him – *HIC HIC* – ever again.'

The teacher patted Jiyoung on the back.

'You know what, Jiyoung? Let me tell you something I've known for a while that you haven't noticed: he likes you.'

Jiyoung was so aghast that she stopped crying. 'He hates me,' she said. 'I thought you said you've seen how he's been treating me.'

'Boys are like that,' the teacher laughed. 'They're meaner to the girls they like. I'll give him a talking-to. Why don't you take this incident as an opportunity to become better friends instead of changing desk-mates on unfriendly terms?'

He likes me? He picks on me because he likes me? Jiyoung was confused. She went over the series of incidents that she had suffered because of him, and still couldn't make sense of what the teacher was saying. If you like someone, you're friendlier and nicer to them. To friends, to family, to your pet dogs and cats. Even at the age of eight, this was common sense to Jiyoung. The desk-mate's pranks made school life so difficult for her. What he'd put her through was awful enough, and now the teacher was making her out to be a bad child who misunderstood her friend.

Jiyoung shook her head. 'No, miss. I really, really don't want to.'

The next day at school, the class was assigned new desk-mates. Jiyoung's new desk-mate was a boy who always sat at the back by himself because he was the tallest, and they did not argue once.

Starting third grade, Kim Jiyoung ate lunch at school twice a week. This was torture for Jiyoung, who was a slow eater. Jiyoung's school was a pilot for the school meal programme, the first in the area to prepare lunch on-site and serve food in the school dining hall. At lunchtime, students marched single-file to the cafeteria in the order of their roster number to eat, and they had to eat quickly so they could clear out and make room for the next class.

While the students who'd finished their lunch ran around the schoolyard like wild horses, Jiyoung shovelled rice into her mouth one big spoonful at a time. Her third-grade teacher was adamantly against them eating small portions or not finishing everything on their trays. Five minutes before their lunch period was up, the teacher would come around banging their metal food trays with a spoon to chastise the students for not eating faster and nag them to hurry up. Every time Jiyoung heard that sound, each bite she swallowed turned into a lump in her throat that refused to go down. The students pushed the remaining food into their mouths, knocking it back with water as if they were taking pills.

Jiyoung was number thirty on the roster of forty-nine. Boys were numbers one to twenty-seven, and girls were twenty-eight to forty-nine. The numbers were assigned in order of birthdays. Jiyoung's birthday was fortunately in April, so she was the thirtieth in her class to get her food, but the girls with late birthdays were only able to sit down to lunch around the time the lower-number students were done. Naturally, the students who were routinely told off for eating slowly were mostly girls.

Then came one day when the teacher was in a horrible mood. The entire class was punished because the blackboard wasn't wiped neatly enough from the previous day, and a surprise fingernail check forced Jiyoung to hide her hands in her desk drawer and give herself a quick trim with a pair of scissors. The ones who were invariably the last to finish their lunch were, as always, anxiously trying to eat faster, and the furious teacher banged on their food trays so hard that grains of rice bounced up to the students' eye level on impact. A few burst into tears with their mouths stuffed with food. The slow eaters gathered around in the back of the classroom during clean-up time after lessons. They arranged a meeting by exchanging gestures, glances and short phrases: *After school today. Youngjin Market. Granny's Tteokbokki.*

The complaints came pouring out as soon as the students got together.

'She's taking something out on us. She picked on us all day over nothing.'

'Yeah, you're right.'

'How can you eat with someone standing over you forcing you to eat, eat, eat?'

'It's not like we're eating slowly on purpose or playing with our food. Some of us just eat slowly! It's not our fault.'

Jiyoung felt the same way. What the teacher was doing was wrong. She couldn't pinpoint exactly what was wrong about it, but she knew that something was unjust and frustrating. But Jiyoung had a hard time voicing her complaints because she wasn't used to expressing her thoughts. She was just nodding at her friends' protestations when Yuna, who'd been quiet until then, spoke up: 'It's unfair.'

'Eating in order of roster number every time,' Yuna explained calmly. 'That's what's unfair. We should suggest that we change the order we eat.'

Suggest to the teacher? Are we even allowed to say something like that to the teacher? Jiyoung briefly wondered, but thought Yuna would be able to pull it off. Yuna did well in school, and her mother was head of the school board. During class meeting time on Friday, Yuna really did raise her hand and pitched the idea.

'I move that we change the order we eat lunch.'

Yuna kept her eyes fixed on the teacher at the podium and reasoned calmly and clearly: getting food in order of roster number means the higher-number students get their food later, and can't help but finish their food later. Eating in ascending order every time is unfair to the higher-number students. The order should change periodically.

The teacher kept a smile plastered on her face, especially the corners of her mouth that were starting to twitch. You could cut the tension in the room with a knife. Jiyoung was so scared for Yuna that her legs were shaking.

The teacher looked back at Yuna for a moment, smiled even harder, and said, 'From next week on, we'll eat in reverse. We'll switch every month.'

The highest-number girls cheered. The order they entered the dining hall changed, but the atmosphere in the hall did not. The teacher still couldn't stand slow eaters, admonished them harshly enough to give them indigestion, and, of the six girls who gathered at Granny's

35

Tteokbokki that day, two remained in the slow-eaters group. Changing the order didn't make that big a difference to Jiyoung since she was thirty out of forty-nine, but she somehow felt that still falling behind would mean defeat for her. So she persevered to eat faster and managed to get out of the slow-eaters group.

A small sense of accomplishment was the reward. They had stood up to a figure of absolute authority and rectified an unfair arrangement. This was a valuable experience for Yuna, Jiyoung and the high-number girls. They developed a bit of a critical eye and confidence, but even then they didn't see why boys came first on the roster. Number one on the roster was a boy, everything began with the boys, and that felt like the right, natural thing. Boys lined up first, boys led every procession no matter where they were headed, boys gave their presentations first, and boys had their homework checked first while the girls quietly waited their turn, bored, sometimes relieved that they weren't going first, but never thinking this was a strange practice. Just as we never question why men's national registry numbers begin with a '1' and women's begin with a '2'.

Class monitors were chosen through direct elections starting from the fourth grade. Elections were held twice a year, once a semester, and all six times from grades four to six, Jiyoung's class had a male class monitor. Most teachers handpicked about five or six smart girls to run errands for them, grade quizzes and check homework. Teachers were in the habit of saying that girls are smarter. Students also thought that girls were smarter, more mature and better with detailed work, but they somehow always elected boys to be class monitors. It wasn't just Jiyoung's class. Back then, there were definitely more boy class monitors. Not long after Jiyoung entered middle school, her mother read an article in the paper that she found astonishing.

'This says lots of girls are class monitors these days. Over 40 per cent![5] When you girls grow up, maybe we'll even have a female president!'

What this means is that less than half the class monitors in Jiyoung's schooldays were girls, and that was actually a great increase from a much lower percentage. And girls were always Head of Class Environment and boys were always Head of Sports in every class, whether they were elected or appointed by the teacher.

When Jiyoung was in the fifth grade, her family moved to an apartment on the third floor of a brand-new building on a bustling street. Three bedrooms, one dining

5 'Girls Can Be School Presidents, Too!', *Hankyoreh News*, 4 May 1995.

and living room, and one bathroom. Their living space doubled, and their level of comfort increased tenfold. It was the result of rigorous saving and careful investing of both parents' earnings. Mother studied the interest rates and benefits of various bank investment plans and invested in workers' asset-building savings, housing lottery savings and fixed-deposit and instalment savings accounts with special benefits. The biggest returns came from the collective private funds she organised with reliable neighbours. But when her relatives, including her sister, suggested organising one together, she flat-out refused.

'Blood relations who live far away are the least reliable. I don't want to lose money and get resentful.'

The former residence was an odd mix of traditional and modern due to years of partial renovations. The dining and living room that was formerly a small courtyard didn't have underfloor heating, and the perfectly tiled bathroom did not have a sink or a tub – just a tap in the wall. The family had to fill a plastic basin then scoop the water with a ladle to wash their face and hair, and throw water on themselves with the ladle to shower. The cramped water closet with a modern toilet was in a separate location by the door. The new place had heating in all the rooms and communal areas, and the bath and toilet were both inside the door, which meant they didn't have to put their shoes on to go to the toilet once they were in the house.

And the girls got their own room. The master bedroom went to the parents and the youngest, the second largest to the girls and the smallest to the grandmother. Father and Grandmother suggested that the girls share with the grandmother as before and give the boy his own room, but Mother was firm. She said that Grandmother was too old to share a room with the girls, that she needed her own space to listen to the radio and Buddhist sutra tapes, and to take naps.

'What does he need a room for?' said Mother. 'He's not even in school yet. He's going to come scuttling into our room with his pillow every night anyway. Do you want to sleep by yourself, or with Mummy?'

The seven-year-old boy strongly insisted he would never, ever sleep without his mummy, and that he had no use for a room. The girls got their own room, as per their mother's plan. Mother had money set aside, without telling Father, to furnish the girls' room. She put two new sets of desks and chairs by the sunny window and a new closet and bookcase by one wall, and gave them each a new sleeping mat, blanket and pillow set. On the opposite wall, she hung a large map of the world.

'See this here? This is Seoul. It's just a dot. A dot. We all of us are living in this tiny, cramped dot. You may not get to see all of it, but I want you to know: it's a wide world out there.'

A year later, Grandmother passed away and the boy inherited her room. But he grabbed his pillow and ran into his mummy's arms to sleep for many years after that.

Adolescence, 1995–2000

Kim Jiyoung attended a middle school that was a fifteen-minute walk from home. Her elder sister, Kim Eunyoung, attended the same school, which was still an all-girls' school when Eunyoung started there.

Even up until the 1990s, the sex ratio imbalance at birth was a serious issue in Korea. In 1982, the year Jiyoung was born, 106.8 boys were born to 100 girls, and the male birth ratio gradually increased, ending up with 116.5 boys born to 100 girls in 1990.[6] The natural sex ratio at birth is thought to be between 103 and 107 boys to 100 girls. The number of male students was already large and obviously increasing, but there weren't enough schools to accommodate them. Co-ed schools already had about twice as many boys' classes as girls', but the high male-to-female

---

6 Statistical Indicators and Ratios in Demography, Statistics Korea.

ratio was a problem, and it didn't make sense for students to be assigned to girls' schools and boys' schools far away when there were schools closer to home. The school became co-ed the year Jiyoung entered, and all other schools in the area followed within a few years.

It was a typical school – small, run-down, public. The school field was so small that the 100-metre sprint track had to be drawn in a diagonal line across it, and plaster constantly crumbled off the building walls. The school dress code was strict, especially for girls. According to Eunyoung, it became stricter when the school went co-ed. The skirt had to be long enough to cover the knees and roomy enough to hide the contours of the hips and thighs. As the thin, white fabric of the summer blouse was rather sheer, a round-neck undershirt was mandatory. No spaghetti straps, no T-shirts, no colours, no lace, and wearing just a bra underneath was absolutely not allowed. In the summer, girls had to wear tights with white socks, and just black tights in the winter. No sheer black tights, and no socks allowed. No sneakers, only dress shoes. Walking around in just tights and dress shoes in the middle of winter, Jiyoung's feet got so cold that she wanted to cry.

For boys, the trouser legs could not be too tight or too loose, but everything else was generally overlooked. Boys wore undershirts, white T-shirts and sometimes grey or black T-shirts. When it got hot, the boys undid a few shirt buttons and walked around with just their T-shirts on during lunch or in between classes. They were allowed to wear dress shoes, sneakers, soccer cleats and running shoes.

One time, a female student who was held up at the school gate for wearing sneakers protested it was unfair to allow T-shirts and sneakers to male students only. The student discipline teacher explained that it was because boys were more physically active.

'Boys can't sit still for the ten minutes between classes. They run outside to play soccer, basketball, baseball, or even *malttukbakgi*. You can't expect kids like that to button their shirts all the way to the top and wear dress shoes.'

'You think girls don't play sports because they don't want to? We can't play because it's uncomfortable to play wearing skirts, tights and dress shoes! When I was in elementary school, I went outside every break to play red rover, hopscotch and skip rope.'

As punishment for the dress-code violation and back-talk, the female student had to do laps of squat walk around the school field. The teacher told her to hold the hem of her skirt together so as not to reveal her under-wear, but the girl refused. Her underwear showed each time she took a step in squat position. The teacher stopped her after one lap. Another student called down to the teachers' office for dress-code violation asked her why she didn't hold her hem together.

'I wanted the teacher to see with his own eyes just how uncomfortable this outfit is.'

The official dress code did not change, but, at some point, the prefects and teachers started to overlook girls wearing T-shirts and sneakers.

There was an infamous flasher who lurked around the school gate. He was a local who'd been showing up at the same time and place for years. He sometimes turned up along the path to school early in the morning and sent the horrified young students fleeing in all directions. On cloudy days, he would appear at the empty lot that directly faced the windows of the all-girls' classroom eight. Jiyoung was in that class in the eighth grade. When girls found out that they were assigned to that class, they shuddered in horror and then later giggled to themselves.

It was early spring not long after the new semester began. Spring showers came before dawn and a thick fog hung around the city all morning. During break after the third period, a girl who was known as the class bully shouted something like a catcall or a cheer out of the window at the back of the classroom. Some of the less 'well-behaved' girls rushed to the window and shouted, 'Mister Flasher! Encore! Encore!' They clapped and laughed their heads off. Jiyoung, whose desk was far from the window, stayed seated and craned her neck, but couldn't see anything. She was curious but too shy to run over and look, and she couldn't work up the nerve to see the flasher with her own eyes. She later heard from her friend who sat by the window that the flasher, encouraged by the girls' response, gave them the show of his life.

The hubbub was instantly silenced when the front door of the classroom flew open and the Head of Student Discipline appeared.

'You there! Screaming by the window! Come out to the front! All of you!'

Everyone sitting by the window was called out to the front of the room. The girls protested – 'We were just sitting in our seats, we didn't shout, we didn't even look out the window' – and the teacher picked five and took them down to the teachers' office. They spent fourth period doing drills as punishment and writing letters of apology. The class bully who returned during lunch spat out of the window.

'Fucking hell. He's the one who stripped! Those dumb fuckers are punishing us instead of catching the pervert? What the fuck did we do? What's there to apologise for? I'm not the one who flashed my junk!'

The girls giggled. The bully spat out of the window a few more times, still furious.

The five girls called to the teachers' office, who were habitually late for school, started coming to school before everyone and slept all through the morning classes. It seemed they were up to something, but they weren't causing trouble of note, so the teachers left them alone. And then it happened. Like enemies running into each other on a bridge, the bully came across the flasher in an alley early in the morning, and the four hiding behind her pounced on him with clotheslines and belts, tied him up and dragged him to a nearby police station. No one knows what happened at the police station or to the flasher. But the flasher was gone for good, although the five girls were suspended. For one week, they weren't allowed to attend classes; they wrote letters of apology in the Student Discipline room next to the teachers' office, cleaned up the school field and toilets, and never talked about what happened.

Sometimes, teachers would give them noogies as they walked by. 'You girls should be ashamed of yourselves. Tsk, what a disgrace for our school.'

The bully hissed 'motherfucker' under her breath once the teacher left, and spat out of the window.

Jiyoung had her first period in the eighth grade. It was neither early nor late for girls her age. Her older sister also got her first period in the eighth grade, and since the two were similar in physical type, diet and rate of growth (the hand-me-downs she received came at regular intervals and fit her perfectly), so Jiyoung had a feeling it was coming. She calmly used one of the sky-blue sanitary pads in Eunyoung's top drawer, and told her sister her periods had started.

'Ugh, your happy days are over,' Eunyoung said. Jiyoung didn't know if she should tell the rest of the family, and, if so, what to tell them. Eunyoung passed on the news to their mother on Jiyoung's behalf. And that was it. Father said he'd be late, there wasn't enough rice in the cooker to go round, and the mother and the three siblings agreed to make three packets of ramen to share and finish off the rice. As soon as a large pot of ramen and four bowls were placed on the dining table, the younger brother filled his bowl to the brim.

'Hey! Leave some for the rest of us!' Eunyoung gave him a noogie. 'And Mother should serve herself first, not you.'

Eunyoung filled her mother's bowl with noodles, soup and an egg, and took half of her brother's noodles. The mother then gave her noodles to her son.

'Mum!' Eunyoung screamed. 'Just eat! From next time on, we're gonna make ramen in individual pots and all stick to our own portion!'

'Since when do you care so much about me? Why are

you so worked up about ramen? And who'll wash all those pots? You?'

'Yes, me. I do a lot of washing and cleaning around here. I put away laundry when it's dry, and Jiyoung helps out, too. There's only one person under this roof who never lifts a finger.'

Eunyoung glared at her brother, and the mother stroked his head.

'He's still a baby.'

'No, he's not! I've been taking care of Jiyoung's bags, school supplies and homework since I was ten. When we were his age, we mopped the floor, hung laundry, and made ramen and fried eggs for ourselves.'

'He's the youngest.'

'You mean he's the son!'

Eunyoung slammed down her chopsticks and stormed off into her room. The mother sighed at the closed door with a conflicted expression on her face, and Jiyoung worried about the noodles getting soft but didn't dare eat.

'If Grandma were alive, she would have ripped into Eunyoung. A girl hitting a man's head!' The youngest slurped his ramen and grumbled. Jiyoung gave him another noogie. The mother did not try to comfort Eunyoung or become angry, but poured another ladleful of ramen soup into Jiyoung's bowl.

'Eat lots of warm food. Dress warm, too.'

One of her friends got a bouquet of flowers from her father when she started her periods, another had a family party complete with cake. But to most girls it was a secret shared only among mothers and daughters. An irritating, painful, somehow shameful secret. It was no different in Jiyoung's family. The mother avoided referring to it directly, as if something that should not be said out loud had happened, as she offered her ramen soup.

Uncomfortable and anxious, Jiyoung lay awake next to her sister that night and calmly went over the things that had happened. She thought about menstruation and ramen. About ramen and sons. Sons and daughters. Sons and daughters and chores. A few days later, she received a gift from her sister: a cloth pouch the size of her palm containing six regular sanitary pads.

Absorbent gel pads and pads with wings did not become common until a few years later. The pads, packed separately at the store in black plastic bags to hide them from view, had a weak adhesive agent, the stuffing bunched in the middle, and they weren't very absorbent. Jiyoung was careful, but blood would leak onto her clothes or bedding when she slept. It was especially more notice-able in the summer when she wore lighter fabrics. Jiyoung would be getting ready for school half-asleep, wandering from the bathroom to the kitchen to the living room to wash, eat and pack her things, when her mother would suddenly gasp and jab Jiyoung in the side to signal her. Jiyoung would then rush into her room as if she'd done something horrible and change.

The discomfort was bearable compared to the cramps. She'd heard about it from her sister and was ready for it, but the second day of her period came with heavy flow and swollen breasts, waist, lower abdomen, pelvis, bottom, and thighs that felt stiff, tight, achy and out of joint. The school nurse lent the girls a hot-water bottle – large, red, filled with hot water and stinking of rubber to boot – but it was as good as a public sign announcing that she was on her period. She tried painkillers that were advertised as being good for 'headaches, toothaches and menstrual cramps', which made her dizzy and nauseous. So she endured the pain. She also harboured an unfounded concern that getting into the habit of taking painkillers for a few days every month would be bad for her body.

As Jiyoung lay on her stomach on the floor to do homework, she clutched her cramping lower abdomen and repeated to herself, 'I don't understand. Half the population in the world goes through this every month. If a pharmaceutical company were to develop an effective pill specifically for menstrual cramps, not the "pain medication" that makes you sick, they would make a fortune.' Her sister filled a plastic bottle with hot water, wrapped it in a towel and passed it to her.

'You're right. In a world where doctors can cure cancer and do heart transplants, there isn't a single pill to treat menstrual cramps.' Her sister pointed at her own stomach. 'The world wants our uterus to be drug-free. Like sacred grounds in a virgin forest.'

Jiyoung hugged the bottle to her stomach and cackled despite the pain.

———

Kim Jiyoung was assigned to a girls' high school about fifteen minutes' bus ride from home. She took extra maths classes at a famous cram school about thirty minutes away, and often hung out at a university area about an hour away by bus. Entering high school meant a sudden expansion of her geographical and social world, which taught her that it was a wide world out there filled with perverts. On the bus and underground, many suspicious hands grazed her bottom and breasts. Some crazy bastards rubbed themselves up against women's thighs and backs. The girls were disgusted by older boys at cram school, church and tutoring sessions pawing their shoulders, stroking their napes and sneaking a peek at their breasts through button-down shirts and T-shirts with low-cut necklines, but the girls couldn't let out a single horrified cry. All they could do was remove themselves from the scene.

School was no better. There were always male teachers who reached up and pinched the soft flesh of the under-arm, patted students on the bottom, or ran their hands down the spine over the bra strap. Her tenth-grade home-room teacher was a man in his fifties, who carried around a pointer that had a hand pointing just the index finger on the tip, which he used to poke girls in the breasts under the guise of drawing attention to missing nametags, or to lift girls' skirts to 'check their school uniforms'. When he left the stick on the podium by mistake one day after morning announcements, one classmate with heavy breasts, whose nametag the teacher often 'checked', marched to the front, threw the stick on the floor, and trampled on it over and over as she wailed. The girls near the front quickly picked up the broken pieces and got rid of them, and her best friend hugged and comforted her.

Jiyoung's situation was better compared to that of other girls who had part-time jobs in addition to school and cram school. Employers harassed them for 'being inap-propriately dressed' or 'not having the right attitude', and held their wages ransom. Customers thought the right to harass young women came with their purchase. The girls stowed away repulsive, frightening experiences with males deep in their hearts without even realising it.

One day, Jiyoung's cram school got out late. By the time she was through with the regular classes and the special seminar, it was quite late. She was standing under the bus-stop sign yawning when a male student made eye contact with her and said hi. He looked familiar but she couldn't place him, so she awkwardly nodded at the boy she assumed to be a classmate at the cram school. He sidled up to her bit by bit. Once the people waiting around them at the bus stop had all gone, she found him standing right next to her.

'Which bus are you taking?'

'Huh? Why?'

'I thought maybe you wanted me to escort you home?'

'You did?'

'Yes.'

'Um, no. I didn't. You can go.'

She wanted to ask who he was and how he knew her, but she was afraid to continue talking with him. She avoided his gaze and fixed her eyes on the car headlights far in the distance. Her bus finally came. She looked away as if it wasn't her bus, and hopped on at the last minute, but the male student managed to follow her on. Peeking at the reflection of the male student's back in the bus window, Jiyoung was frightened out of her mind to think that he was peeking at her, too.

'Hey, are you okay? Are you sick? Here, sit.'

A tired-looking woman who appeared to be on her way home from work offered her seat to Jiyoung, who was pale and drenched in cold sweat. To get help from the woman, she held the tip of her finger and looked desperately at her. The woman didn't understand.

'Do you need me to take you to a hospital?' the woman asked.

Jiyoung shook her head and lowered her hand so the male student couldn't see; she made a fist and opened her pinky and thumb to gesture 'phone'. The puzzled woman looked back and forth between her face and her hand, thought for a while, and then passed her a large mobile phone that she pulled out of her bag. Jiyoung hunched over the phone to hide it, and texted her father: IT'S JIYOUNG MEET ME AT BUS STOP PLEASE HURRY.

She looked desperately out of the window when the bus pulled up at her stop, but her father wasn't there. The male student was standing one step behind her, and the bus door opened. She was afraid to get off, but couldn't keep going to a strange neighbourhood late at night. *Please don't follow me, please, please,* she prayed to herself as she stepped off the bus onto the deserted street, and the male student got off as well. They were the only two around, and the broken streetlight made the bus stop even darker. Jiyoung froze where she stood. The male student approached her.

'You always sit in front of me,' he said under his breath.

'You always fucking smile when you pass me handouts. Always flirting with your hi's and goodbyes and now you treat me like a predator?'

She didn't know who sat behind her, what face she made as she passed handouts to the person behind her, what she said when she passed by someone blocking her way in a narrow hall.

The bus suddenly stopped down the road and the woman from earlier got off. 'Hey! Miss! You forgot your scarf!' she cried as she came running, waving a scarf that anyone could see at a glance a girl of Jiyoung's age would never wear.

'Cunts,' the male student spat and stormed off. When the woman got to the bus stop, Jiyoung collapsed and burst into tears. Her father came running out of the alley. Jiyoung explained what had happened: he might be in her class but she had no memory of seeing him, and he must have deluded himself into thinking she was flirting with him. The woman, Jiyoung and her father sat together on the bus-stop bench and waited for the next bus to arrive. Her father said he came empty-handed because he ran out in a hurry, that he was sorry he couldn't at least give the woman the fare for a cab, and that he would absolutely offer her a reward for her kindness.

'Cabs are worse,' the woman shook her head. 'She must have been scared out of her mind. Console her.'

But that night, Jiyoung got an earful from her father. 'Why is your cram school so far away? Why do you talk to strangers? Why is your skirt so short?' Jiyoung grew up being told to be cautious, to dress conservatively, to be 'ladylike'. That it's your job to avoid dangerous places, times of day and people. It's your fault for not noticing and not avoiding.

The mother called the woman and offered to compensate her, a small gift, or even to buy her a cup of coffee or a bag of tangerines, but the woman refused. Jiyoung felt she should thank her, and called her again. The woman said she was glad Jiyoung was fine, and suddenly declared, 'It's not your fault.' There were far too many crazy men in the world, she'd had her share of run-ins with these people, and the problem was with them, not with the women. Hearing this made Jiyoung cry. Trying to swallow her tears, she couldn't say anything back.

'But you know what?' the woman added. 'There's far more great guys out there.'

Jiyoung quit the cram school. For a long time, she couldn't go near a bus stop after dark. She stopped smiling at people, and did not make eye contact with strangers. She was afraid of all men, and she screamed sometimes when she ran into her younger brother in the stairwell. But she kept thinking about what the woman said. *Not my fault. There's far more great guys out there.* If the woman hadn't said that to her, Jiyoung would have lived in fear for even longer.

The Korean financial crisis of 1997 hit Kim Jiyoung's household. The civil service, known to be the most secure work, was subjected to waves of restructuring. Jiyoung's father, a low-level civil servant who believed downsizing and early retirement only applied to the financial sector and large corporations, was asked to quit. The general consensus among his colleagues was to stick it out no matter what, and he agreed with them. But he was nervous. He didn't make a lot of money, but the fact that he was raising a family was his biggest source of pride. He was a good worker – steadfast, conscientious, always a perfectionist and a model employee – who found himself at a loss and visibly shaken to realise his livelihood was under threat.

Kim Eunyoung was, coincidentally, in the twelfth grade at the time. Unaffected by the tense mood around the house, she kept her grades up. Her practice test results did not improve dramatically, but rose steadily and brought about entrance exam scores she was happy with.

The mother cautiously suggested that her first-born daughter attend a teacher training college outside of Seoul. This suggestion came after a great deal of deliberation on her part. The older generation was being laid off and the younger generation wasn't able to find jobs. Her husband's job, once thought to be completely secure until retirement, faced an uncertain future, there were two other children, and the economy was worsening. For the sake of Eunyoung's future and for the financial stability of the family, the mother wanted her to attend a university that would lead to a high probability of securing stable work. Besides, teacher training colleges had cheaper tuition. But this was after the civil service and education became popular, and the exam score cut-off for teacher training colleges had skyrocketed. Eunyoung had her pick of schools in Seoul, but not the city's teacher training colleges.

Eunyoung, whose dream was to become a television producer, chose journalism as her major and was already looking at previous years' essay test material from the schools she was thinking about. When her mother brought up the idea of teacher training college, Eunyoung said no in a heartbeat.

'I don't want to be a teacher. I already have something I want to do. And why do I have to leave home and attend university so far away?'

'Think ahead. There's no better job for women than a schoolteacher.'

'What's so great about being a schoolteacher?'

'You get off work early. You have school vacations. It's easy to take time off. There's nothing like teaching for working mums.'

'Sure. It's a great job for working parents. Then isn't it a great job for everyone? Why specifically women? Do women raise children alone? Are you going to suggest teaching to your son, too? You're going to send him to a teacher training college, too?'

Growing up, the sisters were never once told by their parents to meet a nice man and marry well, to grow up to be a good mother and a good cook. They'd done quite a lot of chores around the house since they were young, but they thought of it as helping out their busy parents and taking care of themselves, not learning how to be good women. When they were a bit older, the lectures they received from their parents fell under two main themes: a) habits and attitude (sit up straight, keep your desk organised, don't read in the dark, pack your schoolbags ahead of time, be polite to your elders); b) study hard.

Gone were the days when parents thought girls didn't have to get good grades or receive the same education as boys. It had long since been the norm for girls, like boys, to put on a uniform, carry a backpack and attend school. Girls thought about what they would like to do when they grew up, just as boys did; they planned their careers and competed to achieve their goals. This was a time of widespread social support for women's ambitions. In 1999, the year Kim Eunyoung turned twenty, new legislation against gender discrimination was introduced, and in 2001, the year Kim Jiyoung turned twenty, the Ministry of Gender Equality was formed.[7] But in certain pivotal moments in women's lives, the 'woman' stigma reared its head to obscure their vision, stay their hands and hold them back. The mixed signals were confusing and disconcerting.

'Besides, I don't know if I'm going to get married, or if I'm going to have children. Or maybe I'll die before I get to do any of that. Why do I have to deny myself something I want right now to prepare for a future that may or may not come?'

The mother looked up at the world on the wall. On the map with tattered corners were a few green and blue heart-shaped stickers. It was the elder sister's idea to put stickers on the countries they wanted to see. Kim Jiyoung chose the more familiar countries such as the USA, Japan and China, while Eunyoung chose northern European countries such as Denmark, Sweden and Finland. When asked why she picked those places, Eunyoung said she wanted to go someplace with few Koreans. The mother knew what the stickers meant.

---

7 Ministry of Gender Equality and Family.

'You're right,' said the mother. 'I'm sorry I brought it up. You're going to ace that essay test!'

The mother was turning to leave when Eunyoung called, 'Mum, is it because the tuition is cheap? The relative job security? Because I can start bringing home a paycheque right after graduation? Because Father's job isn't a sure thing these days, and I have two younger siblings?'

'That's a big part of it. That's half the reason. The other half is ... I thought a schoolteacher was a really great job in many ways. But now I think you're right.'

The mother answered her honestly, and Eunyoung had nothing to say to that.

Eunyoung started looking into material on elementary-school education, consulted the school careers adviser several times, checked out a teacher training college outside Seoul and brought back an application. The mother was against it this time. She knew better than anyone what it was like to give up on one's dreams for the sake of the family, having made that sacrifice herself. She hardly ever saw her brothers – a sacrifice made without truly understanding the consequences, or even having the choice to refuse, created regret and resentment that was as deep as it was slow to heal, and the bitterness broke up the family.

Eunyoung insisted that wasn't it. She said she'd been more into the idea of becoming a television producer without really knowing what it entailed. That, in fact, ever since she was little, she'd enjoyed reading to her younger siblings, helping them with homework, and doing crafts and drawing with them – schoolteacher suited her better.

'Like you said, Mum, it's a great job. You get off work early, there's school vacations, job stability. Besides, I get to teach things to little children who're as innocent and lively as fresh leaves! How cool is that? Although I'm sure I'll be yelling at them a lot of the time.'

Eunyoung applied to the teacher training college she visited, and was accepted. She got a spot in the dormitory as well. On move-in day, the mother laid out a few essential dorm items and offered advice that fell on the deaf ears of her twenty-year-old daughter bursting with excitement she could hardly contain. The mother came home that day, put her head down on Eunyoung's empty desk and cried for a long time. *She's still a child. I shouldn't have made her leave home so soon. I should have let her attend the school she really wanted. I shouldn't have forced her to be like me.* Jiyoung couldn't tell if the mother felt sorry for her daughter or for her younger self, but she offered her words of consolation.

'She really wanted to go to the teacher training college. She slept with the school brochure. Look – it's falling apart.'

Only after flipping through the brochure with the dog-eared parts worn down and starting to tear did the mother stop her tears.

'You're right.'

'You still don't know her, after raising her for twenty years? You think she'd ever do something she didn't want to? She made the decision because she really wanted it. So don't be sad.'

The mother left the room with a load lifted off her chest. Jiyoung, now alone in the room, felt strange and empty and so elated that she felt she could fly, at least up to the ceiling. She'd never had her own room before. She thought she should get rid of her sister's desk immediately and get a bed. She'd always wanted a bed.

Eunyoung's entering college was a good thing for the whole family.

The father chose early retirement in the end. He still had years ahead of him, but the world had changed too much – while there was a PC for every employee, as a member of the pre-computer generation he still typed with his index fingers only. He'd already reached the number of consecutive years at his job to be eligible for a pension, and his severance pay was a decent sum. He declared it was time for his 'second act' to begin before it was too late. Still, even to Jiyoung, who didn't know much about the world, quitting work at a time when one child had just started college and two younger ones were guzzling money seemed like a risky choice. It made Jiyoung feel nervous, but the mother didn't chastise, fret or dissuade.

The father chose to start a business with the severance money. A work colleague who quit around the same time was starting a China import-export business with his college friends, and asked him to be a partner. The father told the mother that he was going to invest most of his severance money in the business, and the mother was adamantly against it.

'You've worked so hard to support a family of five. Thank you. So now enjoy yourself. Take that money and enjoy yourself. I don't want to hear another word about China. The second you invest, I'm divorcing you.'

As a couple they weren't expressive in their affection for each other, but they went on a trip by themselves at least once a year, and had nights out from time to time, to see a late-night movie or have a few drinks. They'd never had a big fight in front of the children. Each time a big family decision had to be made, the mother advised with caution and tact, and the father generally took her advice. The first thing the father decided unilaterally in twenty years of marriage was the retirement, and now that he was riding the momentum to push for investing in a business, an unbridgeable rift opened up between the mother and father.

The tension between them was still palpable when, one day, the father was riffling through the closet getting ready to go out. He asked where 'that thing' was, and the mother handed him a blue cardigan from the drawer. She found him his black socks when he asked for 'that other thing', and brought him his watch when he asked her to 'hand me that thing'.

'I know you better than you know yourself,' she said as she put the watch on his wrist. 'There are things you are good at, but this isn't it. So drop the China thing.'

The father gave up on the China idea, and said he'd open a business. The mother sold the apartment she had bought as an investment and had let out, and made quite a profit from it. Adding her husband's severance money to this, she purchased a lot on the first floor of a newly constructed commercial building. The price was not low, considering the place wasn't facing the roadside and its location wasn't great, but she seemed to think it was a worthwhile investment. Her reasoning was that the shabby residential areas around the building were being transformed into apartment complexes, and it'd be better to buy a place in a new building rather than renting an existing shop with a premium to pay. They needed a vacant unit to open a business anyway.

The first place they opened was a chicken stew shop. Chicken stew chains were enormously popular in those days, and the father's shop had customers lined up in the street. But the fad didn't last long. He hadn't lost money, but hadn't made much either when it folded and he opened a fried chicken place instead. This was more of a bar that served fried chicken. The father's body, programmed to a lifetime of nine-to-five workdays, aged rapidly due to the late hours he kept. The business folded quickly because of his health issues. The next venture was a franchise bakery, but similar bakeries popped up indiscriminately in the neighbourhood, and a bakery of the same franchise opened up right across the street. The bakeries all failed after a period of more or less equally slow business. The father's bakery held out a bit longer since he didn't have the burden of a monthly rent, but he admitted defeat when a large café/bakery opened nearby.

The atmosphere around the house was about as tense during Jiyoung's last year of high school as it was during Eunyoung's. Amid the scrambling to keep their business afloat in order to secure their children's future, the parents couldn't manage the children's present. Jiyoung spent twelfth grade washing and ironing her and her brother's school uniforms, packing their lunch from time to time, sitting her straying younger brother down and making him study, and getting her own studying done.

Sometimes, when she was so exhausted she felt like giving up, Eunyoung's clichéd words of encouragement – 'Once you get to college, you will lose weight and get a boyfriend' – truly inspired her because Eunyoung actually did lose weight and get a boyfriend in college.

Once the college entrance exam was over, Jiyoung wondered if her parents would be able to afford the tuition fees. She cautiously mentioned shop sales, the father's health and the family bank balance to the mother who'd dropped by at home to make dinner for Jiyoung and her brother. Jiyoung was frankly nervous that bringing up the question of money would prompt her mother to burst into tears, or to tell her to take care of the tuition herself. The mother allayed Jiyoung's fears with five words: 'Get in first, worry later.'

Jiyoung was accepted into the faculty of arts and humanities at a university in Seoul. No one in the family had the time to interfere with Jiyoung's future, so it was the result of her weighing up her options and making the necessary preparations all on her own. Now that she was in, it was time to worry. The mother told her very honestly that they had tuition covered for the first year.

'If things don't change in a year, we'll sell the house or the shop or something, so you don't need to worry about next year, either.'

On graduation day, Kim Jiyoung got drunk for the first

time. Kim Eunyoung took her younger sister and two friends out for *soju*, which Jiyoung found surprisingly sweet and tasty. She drank shot after shot until she passed out and was practically carried home by Eunyoung. The parents shook their heads at Eunyoung for corrupting her little sister, but didn't have much to say to Jiyoung.

Early Adulthood,
2001–2011

Kim Jiyoung was determined to get good grades in college and receive a scholarship, but it turned out to be a pipe dream. Even after perfect attendance, handing in all her assignments on time and studying hard, she only averaged 2.0 in her first semester. She'd maintained good grades in middle school and high school, and she could bomb one test and still pull her grade point average (GPA) up by buckling down and applying herself for the next exam. But in college, it was hard to stand out when in competition with students of a similar level. Without study guides to help decipher the textbook material, or practice test books to help understand the format of the test questions, Jiyoung couldn't figure out how to study for a test.

Gone were the days when students could breeze

through college – no one simply gave up on their GPA and partied for four years any more. Most people kept their grades up, studied English, did internships, entered competitions and worked part time. Jiyoung complained to Eunyoung that there was no romance in college life any more, to which she replied, 'You're out of your mind.'

Many of Jiyoung's college friends told similar stories of their fathers' businesses folding or of them being laid off during the recent financial crisis. While the economy remained bad and college students got by with part-time work and help from parents whose job security still hung in the balance, college tuition fees (frozen during the financial crisis) climbed as if to make up for lost time. In the 2000s, the cost of college tuition increased by over twice the consumer inflation rate.[8]

The first close friend Jiyoung made in college went on leave of absence after her freshman year. She was from a town three hours outside Seoul by express bus. She said she'd worked tirelessly to get away from her parents and go to college in Seoul. She didn't say as much, but it seemed she received little to no financial support from her parents. She said she could work all the part-time jobs she could find and still not make enough to cover tuition, rent and expenses.

---

8 'Repeated Protests Against Tuition Increase', *Yonhap News*, 6 April 2011.

'I teach at the college essay cram school in the afternoon, and waitress at the café at night. I come home, shower, and it's already two in the morning. That's when I prep for class or grade papers before getting a few hours' sleep. As you know, I'm on the work study programme when I don't have classes during the day. I'm honestly so tired I keep falling asleep in class. Trying to afford college is ruining my college life. My GPA is in the toilet, too.'

The plan was to move back home and save money for just one year. Jiyoung lent her an attentive ear knowing nothing could be of comfort or encouragement to her friend besides money. A little over 160 centimetres tall, her friend had lost 12 kilos since starting college, and now weighed just over forty. 'They were right about dropping weight in college!' she cried and laughed her head off as if it was the funniest thing in the world. The elastic around the sleeves of her grey jacket was stretched out, and her bony wrists showed underneath.

Jiyoung's college life was very comfortable by comparison – living under her parents' roof, no student loans and just four hours per week of tutoring work her mother secured for her. Her grades were not good but she found her major interesting, and dipped into a wide range of college academic conferences and joined clubs that would not help her get a job because she didn't have a clear picture of what she wanted to do after college. There were no rewards as instant as pressing a button on a vending machine for snacks, but the activities didn't turn out to be a complete waste of time. Jiyoung discovered that she wasn't as introverted as she'd thought she was when she didn't have the opportunity to think, or form and express opinions. In fact, she turned out to be surprisingly friendly, sociable and fond of being in the spotlight. And she met her first boyfriend at the college hiking club.

He was a physical education major, the same age as Jiyoung. The senior members always paired them together on hikes to help Jiyoung keep up with the group. The boyfriend took her to her first baseball game and soccer match. She didn't understand what was going on all of the time, but the atmosphere in the stadium and her affection for her boyfriend made these sporting events fun. Before the start, he pointed out the major players and important rules of the game for Jiyoung, who knew zilch about sports, and, while the game was in play, they focused on the action. Jiyoung asked him why he didn't explain to her what was going on during the game.

'It's like, you don't explain to me every line and every scene when we see a movie together. Guys who keep explaining things to their girlfriends during the game are,

I dunno, kind of full of themselves. Are they here to see the game, or to show off? Anyway, it's uncool.'

The couple frequented the free film screenings hosted by the college film club, and it was always Jiyoung who chose what to see. He enjoyed all genres – horror, romance, period, sci-fi. He laughed harder and cried harder than Jiyoung did. He got jealous when she mentioned that actor so-and-so was handsome, and made her a CD of all her favourite movie soundtracks.

They usually hung out on campus. They studied together in the library, wrote papers together in the computer lab, and chilled out together in the bleachers in the athletics field. They ate in the student dining hall, snacked in the new convenience store that opened in the student centre, and had coffee in the café next to it. On special days, they would go to a high-end Japanese place or a restaurant out of the average student's price range. He enjoyed listening to Jiyoung retell the plot of a comic-book series she read when she was little, or a novel or popular TV show, and nagged at her to take up exercise – skip rope, whatever.

Jiyoung's mother received information that the new building across the street from their former fried chicken bar was to house a paediatric hospital with wards. She talked her husband – who'd sworn he'd never become an indentured slave of a franchise again – into opening a franchise porridge shop, and a paediatric hospital really did move in across the street and take up floors two to eight. The hospital food was fortunately not very tasty, sending many parents to the porridge shop for takeaways, and families stopped by for a meal on the way to and from the hospital. The apartment complex going up in the area was completed and filled with plenty of young parents who frequently dined out. Even on weekdays, the shop had families drop in for dinner, and families with small children became regulars for lack of other suitable options in the area. The family income was beyond compare to what Jiyoung's father made at the government job.

The family later found out that Jiyoung's mother had purchased a large flat in the massive apartment complex nearby. She'd been paying off the mortgage for years, and, thanks to the porridge business running smoothly, she sold the smaller place they were living in and paid off the last of the mortgage. The family – including Eunyoung, who finished her degree at the teacher training college down south, decided she'd prefer to work in Seoul, and passed the state teacher exam for a position in Seoul – moved into the brand-new apartment.

Jiyoung's father returned home happy after a long night

of drinking with his former colleagues in the civil service, and called his children's names so loudly that the living room shook. The youngest, who was listening to music with his earbuds in and didn't hear him come in, and the two sisters who were asleep came out to greet him, and the father opened his wallet and put cards and cash in their hands. The mother appeared, yawning, and chided him for waking everyone up by coming home uncharacteristically drunk and boisterous.

'My life turned out the best! Those guys at the gathering today can't hold a candle to this! I've made it! Good job, everybody! We've done well!'

As it turned out, the colleague who invested in the Chinese trade blew his severance. The rest were all making a pittance, the ones who stuck with the government job as well as those who retired and opened businesses like he did. He had the largest income and house. Everyone was jealous of his three children, his eldest a teacher, his second attending university in Seoul, and his youngest, a son. As Father stood tall and glowed with pride, Mother linked arms with him and laughed.

'The porridge shop was my idea, and I bought the apartment. And the children raised themselves. Yes, you've made it, but you didn't do it all by yourself, so be good to me and the kids. You smell like rubbing alcohol, so sleep in the living room tonight.'

'Of course! Of course! Half of this is your work! I hail thee, Lady Oh Misook.'

'Half? It's seventy–thirty at the very least. I did seventy. You did thirty.'

The mother yawned again and tossed him a pillow and a blanket, and the father asked his one and only son to sleep out on the living-room floor with him, but was rejected for stinking of alcohol. That didn't dampen his good mood as he wrapped the blanket around him like a cape without washing first, threw himself down on the living-room floor, and shortly afterwards began to snore.

Jiyoung's boyfriend entered the army for his military service after completing his sophomore year. Jiyoung met his parents, and followed him to the training camp and cried her eyes out as she said goodbye, but after only a few months she became unbearably lonely. She would sometimes send letters so long she could hardly stuff them in the envelope, and other times she'd get pissed off for no reason and not answer his call. Always warm and relaxed before he entered the army, the boyfriend was now a tightly wound coil of nerves that unravelled at the slightest provocation. The thought that he was wasting the prime years of his life made him depressed, anxious and angry, in that order. When he came out on leave, save for the sweet moment of reunion, they fought the entire time.

Jiyoung broke up with him. He took it surprisingly well at the time, but drunk-dialled her several hundred times each occasion he came out on leave, texted her in the wee hours – ARE YOU SLEEPING? – and was one time found curled up asleep in front of the porridge shop next to a huge pile of vomit he'd retched up. Rumours spread around the porridge shop building that the second daughter of the porridge shop owner had cheated on her boyfriend in the army and he had deserted his unit to have his revenge.

Jiyoung felt awkward about going back to the hiking club, but stopped in every once in a while to look after the new female recruits. The club was predominantly male, and girls usually left after a few meet-ups. Jiyoung owed her affection for the club to Cha Seungyeon, who swept her under her wings when she first joined the club, and she wanted to pay it forward.

The guys referred to the girls as 'flowers among weeds' and acted as if they worshipped them. No amount of refusal could deter them from carrying everything for the girls; the girls got to choose what to eat from the lunch and post-hike menus, and the girls always got the bigger, better rooms when they went on club trips, even if there was only one girl. But then they claimed it was the camaraderie among good-natured, strong men who can josh around together that kept the hiking club going strong. The president, vice-president and secretary of the club were all men, the club held joint meet-ups with women's university hiking clubs, and there turned out to be a boys-only mountain club alumni group. Seungyeon always said girls don't need special treatment – they just want the same responsibilities and opportunities. Instead of choosing the lunch menu, they want to run for president. Most guys just smiled and nodded, but one devoted member of the club – a guy in the ninth year of his PhD – would always repeat the same thing: 'How many times do I have to tell you? It's too much work for women. You brighten up the club with your mere presence.'

'I'm not here to support you,' Seungyeon would say. 'If the club needs brightening up, get a lamp. God, I'm sick and tired of this place, but I'm gonna keep fighting tooth and nail until the day a woman becomes president of the hiking club.'

That did not happen before Seungyeon graduated, but Jiyoung later heard that a girl who had entered university exactly ten years after her had claimed that seat. Seungyeon's reaction was nonchalant: 'You know what they say – time moves mountains and rivers.'

Jiyoung wasn't as dedicated to the club as Seungyeon, but she kept tabs on the comings and goings until the incident of the junior year autumn club trip. They reserved a place at a nearby nature reserve and, after a quick hike, gathered in small groups playing games, foot volleyball, and drinking. Jiyoung felt chilly, as though she was coming down with something, so went into the room where the new recruits were playing card games with the heater on, burrowed into a pile of blankets and sleeping mats in the corner, and pulled a blanket over her head. The floor heating melted away the tension in her body and she drifted off to sleep, lulled by the sound of club members' voices and laughter.

'Kim Jiyoung's completely done with him, I think.'

Jiyoung heard someone mention her name. *Didn't you have a thing for Kim Jiyoung ... It was more than just a thing ... Well, what are you waiting for, ask her out ... We'll help you out,* came the sound of several voices. She thought it was a dream, but as she grew lucid she gathered who these people were. It was the group of reserve forces returnees who'd been drinking in the living room earlier. She was wide awake now and a little warm, but she couldn't crawl out of the blankets when she was inadvertently eavesdropping on an embarrassing conversation about herself.

'Ew. That's like chewing gum someone spat out,' said a familiar voice.

It was an older member of the club who enjoyed

drinking but didn't force others to do so, and often bought the younger members food, but avoided eating with them lest they felt uncomfortable. She'd always had a good opinion of his level-headed, practical way of handling things. Jiyoung couldn't believe her ears. She listened harder, but couldn't deny that it was him. He could have been drunk. Or perhaps he had said what he'd said to overcompensate for being found out about his feelings for her, and had to say something harsh to discourage the guys from playing matchmaker. She thought of many possibilities, none of which helped to make her feel less devastated. Even the usually reasonable, sane ones verbally degrade women – even the women they have feelings for. *That's what I am: gum someone spat out.*

Drenched in sweat and hardly able to breathe, Jiyoung remained hidden under the blanket. She was afraid of being discovered, as if she'd done something wrong. A while later, when she heard the guys leave the room and the hall was completely quiet, she crawled out of the sauna of blankets and went into the girls' room.

She tossed and turned all night. The next morning, she ran into him while out for a walk on a nearby trail.

'Your eyes are bloodshot,' he said, as warmly and calmly as ever. 'Couldn't sleep?' *No rest for gum! Too busy being chewed and spat out!* she pictured herself saying, but she held her tongue.

The end of Jiyoung's junior year came, and she began preparing for employment in earnest. She'd been retaking the courses she failed in her freshman year to raise her GPA, and her TOEIC score was slowly getting better, but she was still nervous about her future. She had had her heart set on a career in marketing and was looking for internships or corporate-sponsored competitions in the relevant field, but it was hard to get information through her major department because her major had nothing to do with marketing.

She took some classes at the local cultural centre, not so much to learn but to network, and was lucky enough to meet a few people she got along with and with whom she formed something akin to a study group. The group started with three, then someone brought a friend, another left, and the group settled at seven regular members. One of them was majoring in business management at Jiyoung's college. Her name was Yun Hyejin, a year older than Jiyoung but in the same year because she had taken a year off.

The study group members shared information on job opportunities and worked on CVs and covering letters together. They participated in volunteer activities and monitoring of corporations, and applied for internships together. Jiyoung and Hyejin entered several competitions together as a team, and won a few prizes in local government contests and challenges for college students.

During this period, before she started sending out applications and going for interviews, Jiyoung remained hopeful. If the company's philosophy was compatible with her views, and the work was something she was interested in, she didn't care if it was a large corporation. Hyejin was more pessimistic. She was a better candidate than Jiyoung across the board – higher GPA, better TOEIC score, computer skills certificates, a degree in a field companies preferred – but she said she doubted she'd get hired by someone who paid on time, let alone a large company.

'Why do you say that?'

'Because we didn't go to SNU, Korea U or Yonsei.'

'What about the alums who come to the job fairs? People from our college do pretty well.'

'The alums are all guys. How many women have you seen at the job fairs?'

The scales fell from Jiyoung's eyes, and finally she saw. Hyejin was right. Jiyoung had made it to most job fairs or 'meet the alums' events since the beginning of senior year, and she hadn't seen a single female alumnus, at least not at any of the events she attended. In 2005, the year Kim

Jiyoung graduated from college, a survey by a job search website found that only 29.6 per cent of new employees at 100 companies were women, and it was even mentioned as a big improvement.[9] Another survey conducted in the same year showed that, among recruiting managers of fifty large corporations, 44 per cent of respondents chose that they 'would rather hire male to female candidates with equivalent qualifications', and none chose 'would hire women over men'.[10]

According to Hyejin, business management departments sometimes get unofficial recruitment requests either through the department office itself or individual professors, but only male students are recommended. The process was kept so carefully under the radar that it was difficult to ascertain exactly who was recommended to which company for what reason, and if the college recommended only male students or if the company asked specifically for men.

Hyejin told Jiyoung about a girl who graduated a few years ago. She was top of her class for all four years, scored high on foreign language exams, had a spectacular CV including awards, internships, certificates and student club and volunteer activities. There was one company

9 '2005 Job Market with Key Words', *Dong-A Ilbo*, 14 December 2005.
10 'Persistent Discrimination Based on Gender and Appearance in Employment', *Yonhap News*, 11 July 2005.

that she had her eye on, but she found out belatedly that the department received a request for eligible candidates and had selected four male students for interviews (she found out through one of the male students who failed the interview and bellyached about it). The female student filed a strongly worded complaint to her major adviser, asking for the recommendation criteria, and said she would go public with this matter unless she was given a legitimate reason for not being chosen as a candidate. The issue travelled up the chain of command all the way to the department head, throughout which she was given a string of unacceptable reasons: the company seemed to imply a preference for male students; it's recompense for the years they lost serving in the military; they are future heads of households. The most demoralising answer came from the department head himself: 'Companies find smart women taxing. Like now – you're being very taxing, you know?'

What do you want from us? The dumb girls are too dumb, the smart girls are too smart, and the average girls are too unexceptional?

The female student thought it was pointless to carry on with the complaint, and was hired through the company's open recruitment at the end of that year.

'Wow, that's great! So is she still working there?'

'No, she quit after six months or something.'

She had looked around the office one day and realised that there were no women above a certain pay grade. She spotted a pregnant woman in the company dining hall and asked the people at her table how long the company's maternity leave was, and none of the five, including one department head, knew the answer because none of them had ever seen an employee go on maternity leave. She couldn't picture herself at the company ten years down the road and resigned after some thought. Her boss grumbled, 'This is why we don't hire women.' She replied, 'Women don't stay because you make it impossible for us to stay.'

The percentage of female employees who use maternity leave has increased from 20 per cent in 2003 to more than half in 2009, and four out of ten still work without maternity leave.[11] Of course, there are many women who have already left their jobs due to marriage, pregnancy or childbirth, and have not been included in the statistical sample of maternity leave. The percentage of female managers has also increased steadily but slowly from 10.22 per cent in 2006 to 18.37 per cent in 2014, but it's not even two out of ten yet.[12]

'So what's she up to now?'

---

11 Yun Jeonghye, 'Current Use of Parental Leave and Its Implications', *Report on Employment Trends*, July 2015.
12 *2015 Reports on Employment and Labor*, Ministry of Labor, pp. 83–84.

'She passed the law exam last year. The college hung a banner, people were so excited. Did you see it? She was the first from our college in many years.'

'Oh, yeah. I remember. I thought that was pretty cool.'

'Ridiculous, isn't it? "Smart women are taxing," they say. And when she passes the law exam all on her own without any help from the college? They fly banners and toot horns! "Proud alumni!"'

When companies posted open recruitment notices for the second half of the year, Jiyoung felt as though she was standing in a narrow alley clogged with a thick fog, which turned into rain and fell on her bare skin.

Jiyoung wanted to work at a food company, but applied to all companies above a certain size. She did not hear back from any of the forty-three she applied to. She then applied to eighteen smaller but stable places with consistent growth, and did not hear back from them, either. Hyejin sometimes made it to the aptitude test or interview round, but was not offered a position in the end. The two women started applying to every company that was hiring. Jiyoung sent in a covering letter with the wrong company name in it, and passed the application round for the very first time.

Only after Jiyoung was asked to come in for an

interview did she look into what the company was about. It was a toy, stationery and household accessories company that had recently undergone huge growth after negotiating a deal with celebrity agencies to print celebrity caricatures on products. Plush toys, planners, coffee mugs and other unexceptional items were being sold for a huge profit. *A company that steals pocket money from fan boys and girls?* Jiyoung felt conflicted. She wasn't sure if she wanted the job, but grew fonder of the company as the interview date drew nearer, and in the end sincerely wanted the job.

The night before the interview, Jiyoung practised her interview skills with her sister late into the night. It was after 1 a.m. when she put on a thick layer of moisturising cream and went to bed. She lay awake, blinking up at the ceiling, unable to even toss and turn lest the face cream get on her bedding. She dropped off before dawn and dreamed several dreams without endings. She woke up unbelievably tired, and her makeup didn't come out right. On the way to the interview location, she fell asleep on the bus and missed her stop. She still had plenty of time, but hopped in a cab to avoid being lost and anxious right before an important task. The old cab driver with a flawless comb-over glanced at Jiyoung in the rear-view mirror and asked if she was on her way to an interview. She gave him a monosyllabic 'yes'.

'I never take women for my first customer of the day. But I'm giving you a ride because I could tell you were going to an interview.'

Giving me a ride? Jiyoung thought for a moment whether he meant she was getting a ride for free, then figured out what he meant. *Am I supposed to thank the on-duty driver for graciously letting me pay him for his services?* Jiyoung didn't know where to even begin, nor did she want to start an argument that would go nowhere, so she leaned back and closed her eyes.

The three candidates entered the interview room one after the other. The other two were also women of Jiyoung's age. All three had a bob that came down to just below the ears, and wore pink lipstick and a dark grey suit. The interviewers looked over the CVs and covering letters and asked the candidates about their education, posed follow-up questions on lines in their CVs that caught the interviewers' eyes, then moved on to questions about the company, the future of the field and marketing strategies. They were all pretty standard questions the three of them could answer without difficulty. The last question came from a middle-aged male trustee who'd been sitting at the end of the table and nodding without a word up until that point.

'You're at a meeting with a client company. The client gets, you know, handsy. Squeezing your shoulder, grazing your thigh. You know what I mean? Yeah? How will you handle that situation? Let's start with Ms Kim Jiyoung.'

Jiyoung didn't want to panic like an idiot or lose points by being too firm, so she shot for the middle.

'I'll find a natural way to leave the room. Like going to the toilet or getting research data.'

The second interviewee asserted that it was clearly sexual harassment and that she would tell him to stop right away. If he didn't, she would press charges. The male trustee raised an eyebrow and wrote something down, which made Jiyoung flinch.

'I would check my outfit and attitude,' said the final interviewee, who had had the longest to think of an answer, 'to see if there were any problems with it, and fix anything that may have induced the inappropriate behaviour in the client.'

The second interviewee heaved an audible, baffled sigh. Jiyoung was chagrined by the answer, but regret set in as she thought the third woman's answer probably got the most points, and hated herself for thinking that.

A few days later, Jiyoung received an email informing her that she did not pass the interview. Was it because of her answer to the final question? Regret and curiosity lingered for days until she called the HR department and asked. The person in charge said the answer to one question does not determine whether a candidate passes or fails, that it has more to do with whether they have good compatibility with the interviewers, and that perhaps it wasn't meant to be – a by-the-book but comforting answer. Now more relaxed, Jiyoung asked if the other two who interviewed with her had passed. She wasn't holding a grudge or anything, she just wanted to know for future reference, and the HR person balked.

'Honestly, I'm so desperate right now.'

The other two hadn't passed either, came the reply. 'I see.' Jiyoung felt dejected. *If I was going to fail anyway, I should have just spoken up.*

'I would break his fucking arm!' Jiyoung shouted later at the mirror. 'And you! Your question is sexual harassment! And to ask that during a job interview? Would you ask the same question to male candidates?' It did nothing to make her feel better. She would lie in bed frustrated and indignant, kicking off the blankets that clung to her legs.

Jiyoung went to countless interviews after that, where interviewers made references to her physical appearance or lewd remarks about her outfit, stared lecherously at certain body parts and touched her gratuitously. None of these interviews led to a job. She wondered if she should put off graduation. Take a leave of absence, go on a language exchange programme, or do a dozen other things to buy time, but fall semester marched on by and graduating remained her only option.

———

Both her mother and older sister advised Jiyoung not to feel rushed but that was impossible. Yun Hyejin started studying for the civil service exam and suggested Jiyoung join her, but she couldn't decide. The test format wasn't one Jiyoung was confident with, and investing time studying for the exam at that point in her life and, God forbid, failing year after year would mean growing older without work experience and having truly no options in the end. Jiyoung continued to apply for work, lowering her standards in small increments, and in the depths of despair started going out with a guy. When she mentioned it discreetly to her sister, she peered at her for a moment and shook her head.

'In your state? How do you find the emotional energy? Good grief.'

'Beats me,' Jiyoung laughed. In a stressful situation where relationships often break up, she found someone she liked, and that was all there was to it. Outside the window, early snow swirled in the air and reminded her of a poem she read long ago:

Don't I know loneliness, poor as I am?
As I return from saying goodbye to you,
        snow-covered alleys flood with moonlight
        bold and blue.

The boyfriend and Yun Hyejin had been friends since childhood. He was one year older than Jiyoung but still in college after completing his military service. He was more understanding and empathetic of her situation than anyone. He offered no baseless optimism (*You'll be fine!*), impetuous encouragement (*Who cares if you don't get hired right out of college?*), or the usual blaming (*This is your CV? What have you been doing with your life?*). He let her be, helped where he could and bought her a drink if the results were bad.

Two days before graduation, the Kim family was having breakfast, every member present for the first time in a while. The father was debating whether to close the shop for his second daughter's graduation, or at least to open only in the evening, when Jiyoung announced that she would not be attending the ceremony. The father gave her an earful, including the implication that she was 'out of her mind', which had little effect on her. Her nerves were frayed and sensitive only to the words 'We regret to inform you'; no other words or censure could hurt her.

Jiyoung's lack of response to his lecture prompted the father to say, 'You just stay out of trouble and get married.'

That wasn't the worst thing he'd ever said to her, but it was the last straw for Jiyoung, who was holding her spoon upright. Jiyoung was attempting to take a deep breath when an ear-splitting crack, like pickaxe on rock, rang at the table. Her mother, face crimson, had smacked the spoon on the table.

'How can you say something so backward in this day and age? Jiyoung, *don't* stay out of trouble. Run wild! Run wild, you hear me?'

Jiyoung quickly nodded emphatically to calm her hysterical mother through genuine assent. The stunned father broke into a fit of hiccups. That was the one and only time Jiyoung ever saw her father hiccup. One winter night long ago, the family sat around a colander of steamed yams, having bite after bite of the starchy flesh without even a plate of kimchi to wash it down, when the mother, Eunyoung, Jiyoung and younger brother each hiccupped in that order, but not the father. She remembered the family laughing about this. Just as the mermaid princess lost her voice in exchange for legs, do middle-aged men lose their hiccups in exchange for backward ideas? The witch's spell flashed through Jiyoung's mind. Mother's rage put a stopper in Father's twaddle and restored his hiccups.

Later that evening, a marketing agency she'd interviewed for sent her a job offer. Fear, self-reproach and helplessness, brimmed as far as surface tension would allow, turned to tears and streamed endlessly when Jiyoung heard 'congratulations' over the phone. The person most overjoyed by the news was her boyfriend.

The load lifted, Jiyoung and her parents attended graduation and her boyfriend came along. Her parents were meeting him for the first time. They didn't go into the venue where the main commencement ceremonies were held, so they had little else to do besides take a stroll around the campus together, take pictures and find a café to rest their legs and get something to drink. The campus was crowded and noisy everywhere, including the café. The boyfriend ordered four different kinds of coffee, speaking up to be heard over the din, perfectly matched the order with the person, and placed a cute conical napkin fold next to the mother's latte. The father imperiously questioned the boyfriend about his major, place of residence and family, and the boyfriend gave him thoughtful, polite answers. Jiyoung had to keep her head down and bite her lip to stop herself bursting into laughter.

Nothing left to talk about, silence fell over the four

for a moment. The father suggested they get something to eat, and the mother leaned towards the father and muttered something to him. He cleared his throat a few times, gave Jiyoung his credit card and said in a half-rehearsed manner – keeping one eye on the mother for confirmation that he was saying it right – 'It's time for us to go open the shop, so why don't the two of you enjoy yourselves.'

The mother grabbed the boyfriend's hand and said, 'It was so good to meet you. We can't join you, unfortunately, but why don't the two of you get something good to eat, go see a movie, have a nice date, and come by the shop sometime?'

The mother linked arms with the father and dragged him home. The boyfriend bowed so deeply as they walked away his forehead nearly touched the ground. Jiyoung finally exploded with laughter.

'Isn't my mum adorable? She broke up the party, *Oppa*, so you wouldn't feel awkward.'

'Yeah, I figured. By the way, what's the best thing on the menu at your shop?'

'Anything is better than what my mum makes. Mum's not a good cook. But I was raised healthy on store-bought food, takeaways and whatever Mum brought home from the shop.'

The university and the surrounding area were

too crowded, so they got on the tube and went to Gwanghwamun. As the mother suggested, they got themselves a nice meal, saw a movie and dropped by the bookshop to buy a book each. The boyfriend was worried about getting a book on her father's credit card on top of everything else, but she insisted he loved buying books for his kids. In the end, he picked a book he'd had his eye on but couldn't afford. When they climbed the steps up out of the shop, giggling and each clutching a book the size of an encyclopaedia, snow was falling.

Snowflakes fell from the pitch-dark sky, like a gift for each and every person down below. A breeze would sweep across once in a while, scattering the snowflakes every which way. He said if you catch a falling snowflake and make a wish, it comes true, and proceeded to stretch out his hand this way and that, but he missed by a whisker each time. After several tries, he managed to softly land a big, roughly hexagonal snowflake on the tip of his index finger. Jiyoung asked what he wished for.

'I wished that things go well at your first job – not so challenging, not so demoralising, not so exhausting. Maintain good relations with co-workers, get paid without drama, and buy me lots of meals.'

Jiyoung felt as though her heart was filled with snow: replete yet airy, cosy yet cold. She was resolved to handle this next phase well, to keep it less challenging, demoralising or exhausting like her boyfriend said, but at the same time running as wild as her mother hoped she would.

Kim Jiyoung went out to lunch wearing her company ID on a lanyard. Others seemed to be walking around with the IDs dangling at their chests because it was a bother to keep taking it out and putting it away, but Jiyoung did it on purpose. At midday in a busy neighbourhood packed with office buildings, Jiyoung often came across people wearing lanyards with thick straps bearing their company name and a clear plastic case holding their IDs attached to the end, swinging. That was the dream: walking with a group of people also wearing lanyard IDs, holding their purse and phone in the same hand, chatting about the lunch menu.

Jiyoung's company was a fairly large one in the industry, with about fifty employees. The closer to management, the greater the percentage of male employees, but on the whole the office had more women than men. The co-workers were adequately self-sufficient and practical, and the office atmosphere was good. But the workload was considerable and there was no overtime. There were four new employees including Jiyoung – two female, two male. Straight out of college and never having taken time off in her life so far, Jiyoung was a newbie and literally 'the youngest'.

Jiyoung made everyone in her team coffee every morning according to each member's taste, set the table every time they went out to eat, went around with a notepad and took everyone's request when they had to order in takeaways, and cleared their dishes when they were done. It was the team newbie's responsibility to go through news articles each morning, find everything related to the company's marketing clients, do a simple analysis and turn in a report. One day, her team leader went through her report and called her into the conference room.

The team leader, Kim Eunsil, was the only woman among four team leaders. She had a daughter in elementary school, and lived with her mother who took care of all childcare and domestic labour. Some people said Kim Eunsil was awesome, others that she had a heart of stone and still others found the arrangement a credit to her husband. 'Living with the spouse's parents is harder for the husbands than the wives,' they'd say. 'Conflict between married men and their in-laws is becoming a societal problem these days. I don't know him but he must be an obliging person to take in his mother-in-law.'

Jiyoung thought about her own mother, who had lived with her mother-in-law for seventeen years. The grandmother looked after the youngest when the mother went out on hairdresser house calls, but didn't take on any childcare labour such as feeding, bathing or putting the three siblings to bed. She hardly did other domestic chores. She ate food the mother cooked, wore clothes the mother washed and slept in the room the mother cleaned. But no one praised the mother for being obliging.

Team leader Kim Eunsil complimented Jiyoung on her report: 'I've been following your progress. You have a good eye for selecting articles, and your analysis is relevant. Keep up the good work.'

Jiyoung received her first thumbs-up on her first task at her first job. Jiyoung could see this becoming such a great source of strength each time she hit a roadblock in her career to come. A little satisfied, a little proud, but not too obviously gleeful about it, Jiyoung thanked her.

'You don't have to make my coffee from now on,' the team leader continued with a smile. 'Or set my silverware when we go out to eat, or clear my plates.'

'I apologise if I came on too strong.'

'No need to apologise. It's just not your job, Jiyoung. I've noticed this about new employees over the years. The women take on all the cumbersome, minor tasks without being asked, while guys never do. Doesn't matter if they're new or the youngest – they never do anything they're not told to do. But why do women simply take things upon themselves?'

Kim Eunsil had been at the company since there were just three employees. Watching the company and colleagues grow boosted her confidence and pride. The men who were around when she started were now team leaders in marketing divisions of bigger companies, or had started their own firm, and in any case were still working, but none of the female colleagues remained in the field. To be accepted as 'one of the guys', she was last to leave a company dinner, volunteered to work late and go on business trips, and returned a month after giving birth. She was proud of herself at first, but felt conflicted each time female colleagues and women who worked under her left the company, and these days she felt she had done them wrong. In retrospect, company dinners were unnecessary events, and the frequent late nights and business trips were a matter to be resolved by hiring more people. Employees had the right to go on leave or take time off to have and raise children, but she'd unwittingly set a bad precedent. The first thing she did when she became management was get rid of unnecessary company dinners, retreats and workshops. She guaranteed maternity and paternity leave. She said she'd never forget how proud she felt when she presented a bouquet of flowers as a welcome-back present to one of her team members, who returned from a year-long maternity leave for the first time in the company's history.

'Who is she?' Jiyoung asked.

'She left a few months after that.'

The team leader couldn't help out with the frequent late nights and weekends as well. Most of her paycheque went to the babysitter, and even then she was always frantically looking for someone to watch her child at short notice, and fighting with her husband over the phone every day. She came into work with her baby one weekend and ended up throwing in the towel. When the subordinate apologised for quitting on her, Kim Eunsil didn't know what to say.

———

Kim Jiyoung got her first official work assignment. She had to put together a press release based on the results of the home-bedding pollution assessment conducted by an eco-friendly bedding company, and she stayed up several nights writing a two-page report because she wanted to do a really, really good job. The team leader said the report was good. It was good but it read like an article. 'We don't write articles, we write reports that make reporters want to write articles. Please revise,' said the team leader, and Jiyoung stayed up all night again that night. The team leader said the report was good. It was released without major revision, and was picked up by newspapers, a magazine for housewives and even a news network. Jiyoung no longer made coffee for everyone or set the table when they went out to lunch. No one said anything about it.

Work was fun and she liked her colleagues. Reporters, clients and in-house marketing teams from client companies, on the other hand, were another matter. Time, experience and familiarity with the work and field did nothing to make interactions with them less awkward or close the distance between them and her. The marketing agency was hired help to the clients, who were usually older upper-management males, and liked to wave their antediluvian sense of humour in her face. Relentlessly, the jokes kept coming, and Jiyoung could not figure out what the punchline was, or what to say in response. If she laughed, they read it as encouragement to keep going. If she didn't laugh, they asked her if something was wrong.

At a business lunch at an upmarket Korean restaurant, the head of the client company said to Jiyoung, who ordered soybean paste sauce with rice, 'A young person with a taste for soybean paste sauce! I didn't know you were a *doenjangnyeo*, too, Ms Kim! Ha ha!'

Doenjangnyeo, or 'bean paste woman', was a popular Korean portmanteau word among a host of other misogynistic new terms that ended with *nyeo* – woman. Jiyoung had no way of telling if he meant to be funny, or if he was making fun of her, or if he even knew what that word meant. The head laughed, so his staff had to laugh, and since the client was laughing, Jiyoung and a senior member of staff also present smiled awkwardly and changed the subject. So it went.

And then there was the business dinner with the marketing team of a mid-size company. Jiyoung and the team leader oversaw the company's anniversary event from the planning stages to execution and press release distribution, and the client's marketing division invited Jiyoung and the team as a thank you for a job well done. In the cab on the way to the barbecue restaurant in a university area where the client marketing team had already started without them, Kim Eunsil enunciated every syllable, 'I. Really. Don't. Want. To. Go.'

'If they're so grateful, why not send money or presents? Don't they know how awkward it is for us to be in a situation like that? Eat and drink with them as a "thank you for the hard work"? Don't they know we can see right through it? That they want to treat us like servants one last time? God, I hate this. But just one last meal, and that's it.'

The client company's marketing division consisted of the male division head in his fifties, the male assistant divisional manager in his forties, the male section manager in his thirties and the three female staff in their twenties. Three people from Jiyoung's company came: the team leader Eunsil, Jiyoung and Jiyoung's male colleague who helped during the event. The head of the division must have already had a few, for he was red in the face and expressed too much enthusiasm at Jiyoung's entrance. The section manager sitting next to him picked up his beer glass and silverware and got to his feet, gesturing Jiyoung to come and sit next to the division head, who guffawed heartily and complimented 'Mr Han' on his ability to 'read my mind!' Jiyoung felt uneasy and humiliated; sitting next to him was the last thing she wanted to do. She repeatedly insisted she eat with her colleagues, but 'Mr Han' and the assistant divisional manager herded her towards the seat next to the division head. Her male colleague, one of the three who entered the company at the same time she did, couldn't do much for her besides watch nervously. Jiyoung was already seated next to the division head by the time Kim Eunsil arrived on the scene after stopping by the ladies' room first. Jiyoung drank several glasses of beer the division head forced on her.

The division head, newly appointed just three months before after climbing the ladder in the product development division, gave her an unstoppable slew of advice 'coming from experience', including backhanded compliments like, 'You have a nice jawline and attractive nose – just get your eyelids done and you're golden.' He asked if she had a boyfriend, and whipped out filth like, 'No fun scoring when there's no goalie!' and, 'Once women pop, they can't stop!' He wouldn't stop making her drink. 'I've passed my limit, it won't be safe getting home, I'm done,' she said. 'Why so concerned when there's all these guys to escort you home?' *You people are my biggest concern*, she thought to herself as she furtively emptied her glass in the other empty cups and bowls at the table.

A little after midnight, the division head topped up her glass and tottered as he rose to his feet. He hired himself a chauffeur over the phone, speaking so loudly the sound bounced off the restaurant walls, and said to his crew, 'My daughter attends the university right here. She was studying late at the library and wants me to come and pick her up because she's scared to go home by herself. Apologies all round, but I have to go. Miss Kim Jiyoung, finish that beer!'

At that, a frail bit of hope inside Jiyoung crumpled. *In a few years, that precious daughter of yours will find herself exactly where I am now. Unless people like you stop treating me this way.* The alcohol suddenly caught up with her, so she texted her boyfriend to come and pick her up, but there was no answer.

Things quietened down after the division head left. People talked in small groups, a few went out for a smoke, and the one female member of the marketing team took off without a word. Some suggested it was time for a second wave, but Kim Eunsil firmly put her foot down and delivered the three of them safely from the restaurant.

Kim Eunsil left first in a cab saying her mother was sick, and Jiyoung and her male colleague drank coffee from a can under the parasol outside a convenience store. Jiyoung was the one who suggested it, thinking cold canned coffee would sober her up a bit, but leaving the uncomfortable business dinner relaxed her so much she kept falling asleep. In the end, she passed out on the ramen soup-spattered plastic picnic table, and would not get up no matter how much her colleague kicked her under the table and yelled at her.

The boyfriend chose that moment to call her. She was already fast asleep and the colleague picked up to tell him to come and get her, but that was the mistake.

'Hi, I work with Jiyoung.'

'Where is she?'

'She's sleeping, so I picked up.'

'Sleeping? What the hell? Who are you?'

'No! No! That's not what it sounds like! She had too much—'

'Put her on the damn phone!'

Jiyoung made it home safely on her boyfriend's back, but their relationship didn't.

Fortunately, Jiyoung had good colleagues at work and was adjusting relatively well to her first job, which was not as challenging, demoralising or exhausting as she'd braced herself for. And she had bought her boyfriend lots of meals. She had bought him a bag, clothes, a wallet, and sometimes had given him the fare for a cab. The boyfriend, in turn, had spent a lot of time waiting around for her. He had waited for her to finish work, had waited for a day off to spend with her and had waited for her to go on holiday. As the newbie, Jiyoung couldn't decide when to take time off, and the boyfriend had to wait for her confirmation on dates. He had waited for her calls and texts. The amount of time they spent on the phone talking or texting had decreased a great deal after she started work. He had demanded to know why she couldn't shoot him a quick text on commutes, in the toilet, at the restaurant after lunch, or in the minute or two between tasks. It wasn't that she didn't have time – she didn't have room in her head for other thoughts. Many office worker–college student couples she knew had the same problem. It didn't matter if the office worker was the guy or the girl.

Jiyoung already felt guilty that she couldn't be of help to her boyfriend, who was now in the last year of college preparing for employment. She remembered very clearly just how supportive he'd been when she was in his shoes. When she thought back to those days, she still felt so in love that she ached. But her daily life was a battlefield and she didn't have the luxury of being able to cater to someone else's well-being when she was at risk of getting bloodied if she let down her guard. Disappointment collected between them like dust on top of the refrigerator or medicine cabinet – spots clearly visible but neglected. They had been drifting apart when the convenience store pass-out incident sparked a huge fight.

He knew that this was the first time Jiyoung had drunk at a business dinner until she passed out, that she'd been forced to drink, and that there was nothing going on between her and the guy who picked up the phone. He knew very well, but that didn't matter. Onto the feelings left unsaid for so long that they were desiccated and crackling, a tiny spark of a flame fell and instantly reduced the most shining romance of youth to ashes.

Jiyoung was set up with a few people after that, and went on second dates with some of them. The guys were all much older, more advanced in their careers, and probably had higher annual incomes. They paid for meals, movie and theatre tickets, and gave her gifts small and big, like Jiyoung used to give her boyfriend. But she didn't feel close to any of them past a certain point.

———

The company was putting together a planning team. The dynamic so far had been to find clients through sales pitches and do the clients' bidding, but now the time had come for the company to plan ad campaigns and recruit clients to work with. This was to become a long-term project, not a one-time thing. The company had reached an impasse where the limitations of a marketing agency left them in the position of hired help passively waiting around for work to come. The planning team, if not immediately successful, could establish a more pro-active position with the clients, thus generating a steadier revenue stream and greater growth. Most people in the office were intrigued by this new venture, and Jiyoung was no exception. She let Kim Eunsil, who was to lead this new team, know that she was interested in joining the planning team.

'Yeah, you'll be good at it,' came the positive response, but she didn't make the team in the end. Three people from middle-management section managers known for their competence and the two male colleagues who started at the same time as Jiyoung were assigned to the planning team. The company treated the planning team like an elite squad, which made Jiyoung and the other, female employee who started with her, Kang Hyesu, feel robbed. Since the beginning, the two of them had established a good reputation at work. The older mem-bers openly joked that they hired the two men and two women at the same time with the same criteria and yet the two guys had a steeper learning curve ahead of them.

The guys weren't bad at their jobs, but they did handle the easier clients.

The four of them had been very close, and had never encountered any unpleasantness in spite of their very different personalities, but an odd rift had formed among them since the two guys moved to the planning team. The group chat, which had buzzed constantly throughout the working day, went quiet. Their brief, secret coffee breaks together, lunch rendezvous and regular bar nights also came to an end. When they ran into each other in the hall, they tried not to make eye contact and acknowledged each other with awkward nods. Kang Hyesu, the eldest of the four, had finally had enough and organised a bar night.

They drank pretty late into the night, but no one was drunk. Their bar nights had been casual meet-ups full of dumb jokes, whingeing about work, and giggling and gossiping about members of their respective teams, but the mood that evening was very serious from the start, thanks to Kang Hyesu opening up about her brief office romance.

'It's finished now. For God's sake don't ask me who it was, don't make assumptions and don't mention this to anyone. I'm dying inside these days. Console me.'

In her mind, Jiyoung flipped through the Rolodex of single guys in the office until the thought that he may not necessarily be single brought on a sudden migraine. The two guys chugged their beer. One of them opened up about his worries over his younger brother who had graduated last year and had not been able to find a job. He was still paying off his student loans, and wasn't sure his younger brother, who had an even bigger amount to pay off, would ever be out of debt.

'Is it confession night?' the other asked, scratching his head. 'I'll go. Honestly, I don't think I belong on the planning team.'

Jiyoung discovered a lot of things that night. The planning team was hand-picked by the head of the company himself. The competent middle-management section managers were chosen because the planning team needed a strong foundation, and the men were picked because the planning team was a long-term project. The head of the company knew that the nature and intensity of the marketing agency job made it difficult to maintain a decent work–life balance, especially if childcare came into play, and therefore he did not think of female employees as prospective long-term colleagues. He had no intention of giving employees better hours and benefits, either. He found it more cost-efficient to invest in employees who would last in this work environment than to make the environment more accommodating. That was the reasoning behind giving the more high-maintenance clients to Jiyoung and Kang Hyesu. It wasn't their competence; management didn't want to tire out the prospective long-term male colleagues from the start.

Jiyoung was standing in the middle of a labyrinth. Conscientiously and calmly, she was searching for a way out that didn't exist to begin with. Baffled and ready to give up, she was told to try, try again; to walk through walls if it came to that. Revenue drives a businessman, and you can't blame someone for wanting maximum output with minimum input. But is it right to prioritise short-term efficiency and balance sheets? Who'll be the last ones standing in a world with these priorities, and will they be happy?

She also learned that the guys were paid better from the very start, but that information stirred very little in Jiyoung, who'd filled the day's quota of shock and disappointment. She wasn't confident she could follow the upper-management and senior members' lead and trust that working hard was the answer, but when morning came and the alcohol had worn off, she found herself heading to the office as if out of habit. She handled the tasks she was given as usual. But her drive and faith had undoubtedly been weakened.

The gender pay gap in Korea is the highest among the OECD countries. According to 2014 data, women working in Korea earn only 63 per cent of what men earn; the

OECD average percentage is 84.[13] Korea was also ranked as the worst country in which to be a working woman, receiving the lowest scores among the nations surveyed on the glass-ceiling index by the British magazine *The Economist*.[14]

13 Gender Wage Gap, 2014, OECD.
14 'The Best and Worst Places to Be a Working Woman', *The Economist*, March 2016.

Marriage, 2012–2015

The parents of the bride- and groom-to-be met for the first time at a nice Korean restaurant in Gangnam close to the bus terminal. 'Nice to meet you, you must be exhausted from the long trip,' and other niceties were followed by a sheepish silence. Jung Daehyun's mother suddenly began to compliment Kim Jiyoung, whom she'd met only twice. *She's level-headed, amiable and sensible. She remembered that I didn't drink coffee and brought me herbal tea the next time we met, and noticed just by talking on the phone that I was coming down with a cold.* The herbal tea was recommended by the department-store assistant based on the price range Jiyoung set, and she'd said something about a cold because it was the time of year when seasons changed and many people came down with the flu. She hadn't noticed anything different about her voice. It stressed Jiyoung out to know that her meaningless actions could be interpreted in so many ways.

'You're too kind,' Jiyoung's mother replied, smiling proudly, happy to hear the future mother-in-law praise her daughter. 'She's all grown-up, but she doesn't really know much about keeping a home.'

She joked as if to make excuses – 'My daughters never had the opportunity to learn – it's my fault for not being able to leave chores unattended – but they won't starve themselves, will they?' – and Daehyun's mother agreed. The two mothers went on for quite a while about how their daughters only studied and worked without ever helping out around the house.

'Everyone fumbles in the beginning. You get better with practice. Jiyoung will handle it well,' Daehyun's mother concluded.

No, I don't think I'll handle it well, Jiyoung thought to herself. Oppa *knows more about housework from living by himself for years, and he said he'd take care of everything when we get married.* But both Jiyoung and Daehyun only smiled.

Adding their savings to Daehyun's bachelor studio *jeonse* deposit plus a small loan, the couple signed a lease for an 80-square-metre apartment, bought furnishings and paid for the wedding and honeymoon. Thanks to Daehyun's large deposit and their more or less frugal attitude towards money, they could get married without asking their parents for help. Each started work around the same time and Jiyoung did not have to pay rent and utilities since she lived with her parents, but Daehyun had saved much more. This did not come as a surprise to Jiyoung because his income was higher, he worked for a bigger company, and marketing was known to be an underpaid sector, but when she realised just how much more he'd been able to save, she felt a little demoralised.

Married life was better than expected. Both got off work late and often worked weekends, which meant there were many days when they couldn't so much as have one meal together. But they went to see late-night screenings sometimes, ordered in at night, and, on weekends when neither had to work, they slept in and watched movie info shows while eating toast Daehyun made. Days like that felt like a date or playing house.

On the Wednesday that marked the one-month anniversary of their wedding ceremony, Jiyoung caught the last train home from work, and Daehyun came home unusually early, made himself ramen, did the dishes, cleaned out the fridge and folded laundry while watching a TV show. When Jiyoung walked in, he was waiting for her with a piece of paper on the dining table. It was the form to legally register their marriage. He'd downloaded and printed it out at work and had two guys from work sign as witnesses. Jiyoung couldn't help but laugh.

'What's the rush? We had a wedding and we live together. Nothing will change because of one document.'

'It changes how we feel.'

Jiyoung had been oddly moved that he was in a rush to make the marriage legal. She'd felt good, good and elated and buoyant, like something lighter than air was filling her up in the lungs or stomach. Daehyun's answer to her question pricked her heart like a short, fine needle and made a microscopic hole. The air escaped slowly, little by little, and brought her back down. She didn't think legal procedures changed how she felt. Was Daehyun more committed for wanting to make the marriage legally binding, or was she more dedicated for thinking she'd always feel the same whether they were official or not? Jiyoung saw her husband in a new light – more dependable, yet oddly more alien.

The couple filled out the paperwork at the dining table in front of their laptop. Daehyun drew each stroke, glancing at the laptop to write down his place of family origin on the form, and Jiyoung was no better. She was probably writing the Chinese character for her family origin for the first time. Daehyun had asked both sets of parents for their information beforehand, and they filled out that section without difficulty. Then came section five: 'Do you agree that your child will take his or her mother's surname and place of family origin?'

'What do you want to do about this?'

'About what?'

'Number five here.'

Daehyun read the question out loud, looked at Jiyoung and casually said, 'I think "Jung" is a decent surname.'

In the late 1990s, the dispute over the *hoju* system (the traditional family registration scheme, in which all members of a family must be registered under the patriarch) began in earnest with the emergence of organisations arguing for its abolition. Some people publicly used both of their parents' surnames, and a few celebrities revealed their painful childhood memories of being picked on for having a different family name to their fathers. At the time, a very popular TV show about a single mother at risk of losing custody of her child, whom she'd been raising all on her own, to a deadbeat dad taught Jiyoung about the absurdity of the *hoju* system. But there were still those who thought its abolition would turn blood relations into strangers and make Korean society savage.

The *hoju* system was finally abolished in January 2008 and replaced with a new law. This was possible after the Constitutional Court found *hoju* incompatible with the constitution's gender equality clause in February 2005.[15] Today, there is no such thing as 'family registry', and people are living their lives with the new individual identification system. It's not compulsory for a newborn to take the patriarch's last name any more, and a couple has the option to decide – upon signing their marriage registration – to give the mother's surname and family origin to their children. Technically, it is possible, but there have been only 200 cases in which children took their mother's name since the abolition of the *hoju* system in 2008.[16]

'Most people still take their father's last name. People will think that there's some story behind the kid if they have their mother's last name. There will be a lot of explaining and correcting and confirming to do if the child takes the mother's last name,' Jiyoung said and Daehyun nodded.

Jiyoung did not feel good as she checked 'NO' with her own hand. The world had changed a great deal, but the little rules, contracts and customs had not, which meant the world hadn't *actually* changed at all. She mulled

---

15 'The Abolition of *Hoju* System: Overcoming Barriers to Equality', *Policy Report of Roh Moo-hyun Administration*, 2008.
16 'Can My Last Name Decided by My Parents Be Egalitarian?', *Women's News*, 5 March 2015.

over Daehyun's idea that registering as legally married changes the way you feel about each other. Do laws and institutions change values, or do values drive laws and institutions?

———

Parents on both sides were waiting for 'the good news'. Parents, uncles and aunties kept having 'auspicious dreams', prompting them to call Jiyoung the next morning to ask after her. A few months passed, and they began to suspect solicitously that Jiyoung had health problems.

For the first celebration of Daehyun's father's birthday after their wedding, the couple went down to Busan to have lunch and be introduced to close relatives who lived in the area. As they made, ate and cleared lunch, the topic of conversation among the family elders was whether Jiyoung had 'good news', why not, and what they were doing to get pregnant. Jiyoung said they weren't planning on having children yet, but the elders were convinced, regardless of Jiyoung's input, that she *couldn't* get pregnant, and proceeded to investigate. *She's too old … She's too skinny … Her hands are cold … She must have bad circulation … The zit on her chin is a sign of an unhealthy uterus …* They concluded the problem was her.

'What are you doing, sitting on your hands,' one of

the aunts leaned towards Daehyun's mother. 'Get your daughter-in-law a box of herbal medicine for fertility! Jiyoung must feel hurt by your lack of concern!'

Jiyoung did not find the 'lack of concern' hurtful. These conversations, on the other hand, were unbearable. *I'm healthy, I don't need medicine. Family planning is between me and my husband, not relatives-in-law I've never met in my life.* She held in these words and said, 'No, no, it's okay.'

The couple fought the entire drive back from Busan to Seoul. Jiyoung was sincerely hurt that Daehyun hadn't said a word while his family treated her like she had some big physical issue, and he said he had kept his mouth shut so as not to ruffle feathers and blow the problem out of proportion by taking her side. She couldn't understand his logic, and he said she was overreacting. She was saddened that he was dismissing her feelings as an overreaction, and the explanations he came up with turned into more ammunition for her to criticise him.

They drove straight back without making a single stop, and when the car was parked in the basement lot of their apartment building, Daehyun broke the long silence.

'I thought about it all the way back, and I think I should defend you when my family's being unfair to you. Because I'm more comfortable with them than you are. When we're with your family, you speak on my behalf, too. How about that? I apologise for what happened today. I'm sorry.'

Due to Daehyun's sudden change of attitude, Jiyoung could no longer express her anger at him. She meekly accepted his apology, as if she'd done something wrong.

'And there is one way to stop my parents' nagging for good.'

'What?'

'Let's just have a kid. If we're going to have one eventually anyway, why not avoid the lectures by just having one? We're not getting any younger.'

Daehyun's suggestion sounded as blithe and casual as, 'Let's try the Norwegian mackerel' or, 'Let's do a puzzle of Klimt's *The Kiss*.' At least that's what it sounded like to Jiyoung. The couple had not yet had a conversation about family planning or when to have a child, but both believed that having children is the natural next step after marriage, and it was hard to argue with what Daehyun said. But having a child was not so casual a decision for Jiyoung.

Her sister, who had married a year earlier, did not have a child, and neither did most of her friends who had also married late, so Jiyoung had never had close contact with a pregnant woman or a newborn infant. She couldn't gauge what about her body would change and to what degree. Most importantly, she wasn't sure if she could take on both childcare and her career. Daycare centres and babysitters would not be enough, as the couple always worked late and on weekends. Their respective parents were in no position to help out. Then she felt awful that she was already thinking about putting her child in someone else's care when it wasn't even born yet. Why were they thinking of having a child they would never have time for, who would always make them feel like disappointments as parents? Watching Jiyoung agonise, sigh after sigh, Daehyun patted her on the back.

'I'll help out. I'll change the nappies, do the feedings and boil the babygrows.'

Jiyoung explained to the best of her ability how she felt: anxious as to whether she'd be able to keep her career after having a baby, guilt over already thinking about having someone else look after their child. Daehyun listened attentively and nodded at the appropriate moments.

'Still, think about what you'll be gaining, not just what you'll be giving up. Think how meaningful and moving it is to be a parent. And if we really can't find someone to look after the child, worst-case scenario, don't worry about quitting your job. I'll take care of us. I won't ask you to go out and make money.'

'And what will you be giving up, *Oppa*?'

'What?'

'You said don't just think about what I'll be giving up.

I'm putting my youth, health, job, colleagues, social networks, career plans and future on the line. No wonder all I can think about are the things I'm giving up. But what about you? What do you lose by gaining a child?'

'Me? Well ... I ... Things won't be the same for me, either. I won't get to see my friends as often because I'll have to come home early. I'll feel bad about attending business dinners or working late. It'll be tough to come home and help out with chores after working all day. And besides, you know, I'll have you and our child. Financial support! As the head of the household. Financial support! That's a huge responsibility.'

She tried not to react emotionally to his words, but it was difficult. His list of potential losses seemed like such a trifle compared to the way her life could be thrown off course.

'You're right. Raising a child will be hard for you, too. But I have a job because it's fun and I enjoy it – the work and making money – not because *Oppa* wants me to go out and make money.'

As hard as she tried not to, she couldn't help feeling she was bargaining something away.

One weekend morning, the couple went for a walk in the nearby arboretum. A mysterious white grass covered the arboretum grounds. Daehyun asked if there was such a thing as white grass, and Jiyoung said it looked like a kind of herb. They walked across a meadow, treading softly on the thick grass. In the middle of the meadow, they came across a round, green thing about the size of a child's head sticking out of the earth. They went closer and saw that it was a radish. A large, shiny radish was half buried in the ground. Jiyoung reached down, grabbed the radish and pulled. Out came a sleek radish with hardly any dirt on it.

'Isn't that a re-enactment of that children's story about a radish?' Daehyun said and laughed. 'What a strange dream.'

Jiyoung had the worst morning sickness – the merest gulp of air mid-yawn could make her retch – until the very end of her pregnancy. She was more or less fine apart from that. No complications, swelling or dizziness, but she had indigestion, constipation that made her feel bloated and the occasional shooting pain in her lower back. She was easily exhausted and, worst of all, very drowsy.

For safety reasons, the company allowed pregnant employees to push their work hours back by half an hour. When she announced her pregnancy at work, one of her male colleagues exclaimed, 'Lucky you! You get to come to work late!'

Lucky me, I get to retch all the time, am unable to eat or shit properly, and I'm always tired, sleepy and sore all over, Jiyoung wanted to say but held it in. She was disappointed by his insensitive remarks, which showed no concern for all the discomforts and pains of pregnancy, but she couldn't expect someone who wasn't her husband or family to understand that.

When Jiyoung fell quiet, the other male colleague chided, 'But she goes home thirty minutes late. She has to work the same amount in the end.'

'Yah! As if anyone in this office gets to go home on time! She's just getting thirty minutes for free!'

Jiyoung, out of anger, said she had no intention of coming in half an hour late. That she would be keeping the same hours as everyone else. That she didn't intend to get a single minute for free. She wished she hadn't spoken so rashly as she came into the office an hour ahead of everyone else to protect her pregnant self from the rush-hour metro hell. She wondered if she was setting a bad precedent for the younger women in the office. She couldn't win: exercising all the rights and utilising the benefits made her a freeloader, and fighting tooth and nail to avoid the accusation made things harder for colleagues in a similar situation.

When she took the underground during the day for a meeting or took a half-day for a doctor's appointment, people often gave up their seats for her, but not during rush hour. Squeezing her side to manage the splitting pain, she told herself that people did care – they were just too tired to act on it. But she was honestly hurt when people gave her an uncomfortable or dirty look just for standing in front of them.

On the tube home from the office one day, slightly later than usual, there were no empty seats and hardly any free handles to hold onto in the carriage. She managed to grab a free handle near the doors when a woman who looked fifty-something glanced at her belly and asked her how far along she was. She smiled awkwardly and mumbled something so as to not draw attention to herself. The woman asked if she was on her way home from work. Jiyoung nodded and looked away.

'I'll bet your sides are starting to hurt, huh? Knees and ankles, too? I sprained my ankle last week on a hike. It hurts even now, I'm not putting any weight on it. Otherwise I'd have given you my seat. Gosh, I wish someone would give up their seat for you. Hang in there, mama.'

The woman looked around for someone to shoo off their seat, making everyone uneasy, but not as uneasy as Jiyoung. She said over and over that she was fine, that she didn't need to sit, but the woman wouldn't hear of it. Jiyoung was about to get away from her when the girl in a university jacket sitting next to the woman jumped to her feet agitatedly.

As she knocked into Jiyoung's shoulder and pushed past her, she said loud enough for Jiyoung to hear, 'About to pop and still taking the tube to go make money – clearly can't afford a kid.'

Tears fell from Jiyoung's eyes. That's what I am: someone who still goes to make money. By taking the tube. When I'm about to pop. Tears too heavy to hide or cover up kept on coming. She hopped off the train at the next stop. She sat on a bench on the platform and cried and cried, and then came out through the turnstiles. She was far from home and in an area she'd never been to, but she left the station. She found a queue of cabs on the rank, and got into the first one. She could have caught the next train home and cried in the tube carriage where she didn't know anyone, but she panicked and got off. She chose to take a cab. She wanted to.

The obstetrician with a belly slightly bigger than Jiyoung's smiled warmly and informed her to 'buy pink baby clothes'. The couple didn't have a preference, but they knew the family elders were expecting a boy, and a small sense of dread came over them to think of the stressful situations that might occur the moment the parents found out it was a girl. Jiyoung's mother said, 'It's okay, the next one will be a boy.' Daehyun's mother said, 'I don't mind.' Jiyoung very much minded what they'd said.

It wasn't just the older generation. Women of Jiyoung's age shamelessly said things like: 'My first was a girl, so I was nervous until I found out the sex of the second one'; 'I can hold my head up high around my in-laws now that I have a boy'; or, 'I started getting myself all kinds of expensive food when I found out I was having a boy.' Jiyoung wanted to say she could hold her head up high, too. That she was eating everything she was craving, but she held back so as not to sound bitter.

As the due date closed in, Jiyoung debated back and forth between maternity leave and quitting work altogether. The sensible course was to take as long a maternity leave as possible and weigh her options in the meantime, even if the best idea turned out to be quitting, but, from the company and her colleagues' point of view, that wasn't ideal.

The couple discussed this matter very thoroughly. On a large sheet of paper, they wrote down three scenarios: going straight back to work, going back to work after a year of maternity leave and not going back to work at all. For each scenario, they discussed who would be in charge of childcare, how much it would cost, and other pros and cons. As long as they both worked, the only option would be to send the child to Daehyun's parents in Busan, or get a live-in nanny.

The Busan option wasn't feasible. The parents said they would gladly raise her, but they were both elderly and his mother had recently had surgery on her back. The couple was reluctant to get a live-in nanny. She would not just take care of the child, but share in their everyday routine, household things and time with the family. *It's hard enough finding someone who's good with childcare – would it be possible to find a stranger who would get along with us, too? Even if we found someone suitable, the cost would be considerable. And how long would the nanny be with us? What would be the appropriate age for a child to go to school, go to after-school activities and get her own dinner? And how many close calls, nerve-racking situations and moments of guilt would we have to live through until then?*

In the end, they concluded that one of them had to be a stay-at-home parent, and that one person, of course, was Jiyoung. Daehyun's job was more stable and brought in more money, but, apart from that, it was more common for husbands to work and wives to raise the children and run the home.

The fact that Jiyoung saw this coming did not make her feel any less depressed. Daehyun patted her on her slouched back.

'We'll get a sitter once in a while when our baby's bigger, and send her to daycare, too,' he said. 'You can use that time to study and look for other work. Think of this as an opportunity to start a new chapter. I'll help you out.'

Jiyoung knew that Daehyun was being sincerely supportive, but she still couldn't hold back her anger.

'Help out? What is it with you and "helping out"? You're going to "help out" with chores. "Help out" with raising our baby. "Help out" with finding me a new job. Isn't this your house, too? Your home? Your child? And if I work, don't *you* spend my pay, too? Why do you keep saying "help out" like you're volunteering to pitch in on someone else's work?'

Jiyoung felt bad about jumping down his throat after the two of them had done a good job of making a tough decision together. She apologised to her stunned, stuttering husband, and he said, 'No worries.'

Jiyoung didn't cry when she told the head of the company that she was quitting, or when team leader Kim Eunsil said she hoped to work with her again in the future. She didn't cry as she brought her things back from the office a little at a time every day, or at the farewell party, or on her final commute home. The day after she left, she made Daehyun warm milk and saw him off, crawled back into bed and woke up around nine. *I should get myself toast on the way to the tube station. I'll get* biji *soup for lunch at the Jeonju Diner. Maybe catch a movie before I head home if I get off work early? I have to stop by the bank to withdraw the matured savings account.* Then it suddenly hit her that she didn't have an office to go to any more. Her daily routine would be different from now on, and, until she got used to it, predicting and planning would be impossible. That's when the tears came.

The marketing agency was her first workplace. Her first step into the working world. People said that the professional world was a jungle and that the friends you make after college aren't real friends, but that wasn't necessarily true. Things were more absurd than sensible, and the company was a place where one reaped far less than one sowed, but, being an individual who did not belong to any group, Jiyoung realised that the company had been a fortress for her. There were more good colleagues than bad. She got on better with them than she did with her college friends, perhaps due to similar interests and tastes. The job did not pay well or make a big splash in society, nor did it make something one could see or touch, but it had brought her joy. It afforded her a sense of accomplishment when she completed tasks and climbed the ladder, and gave her a sense of reward knowing she was managing her own life with the money she earned. But that was all over now. That's how it turned out, even though she wasn't incompetent or lazy. Just as putting the care of your child in another's hands doesn't mean you don't love your child, quitting and looking after your child doesn't mean you have no passion for your career.

In 2014, around the time Kim Jiyoung left the company, one in five married women in Korea quit their job because of marriage, pregnancy, childbirth and childcare, or the education of their young children.[17] The workforce participation rate of Korean women decreases significantly before and after childbirth. Its percentage starts at 63.8 for women aged between twenty and twenty-nine, drops to 58 per cent for women aged thirty to thirty-nine, and increases again to 66.7 per cent for women over forty.[18]

Well past the due date and with no sign of her going into labour, Jiyoung and the doctor agreed the best option was for her to be induced, as the baby was getting larger and the amniotic fluid was running low. The night before going into hospital for the birth, Jiyoung and Daehyun shared grilled pork belly for four, had a bowl of rice each, and then went to bed early. Jiyoung couldn't sleep. She was scared and curious and visited by insignificant memories from the past, like her older sister doing her homework for her, her mother forgetting to put pickled radish in

---

17 'Women's Lives Through Statistics in 2015', Statistics Korea.
18 Choi Minjeong, 'Current Situations and Tasks of Policy for Supporting Women on Career Breaks', *Health and Social Welfare Review*, September 2015, p. 63.

her school picnic *kimbap*, her work colleague bringing her plain rice puffs at the height of her morning sickness. As the memories popped up one after another, the emotions and sensations she felt at the time came rushing back in rich detail. It was close to dawn when she finally fell asleep, and had several dreams of giving birth during the brief repose.

Jiyoung checked into the hospital early and changed into hospital clothes. On the hospital bed in the pre-delivery room, she was given an enema and labour induction treatment with a foetal movement monitor strapped around her belly. Now her eyelids grew heavy and she started dozing off, but was woken up every time by two nurses and one doctor who took turns coming in to perform cervical examinations. The rounds took 'check-ups' to a new level for Jiyoung. If they'd reached in, grabbed the baby by the hand and pulled her out, it couldn't have felt more intrusive. It felt to Jiyoung like a natural disaster akin to a hurricane or an earthquake was happening inside her. The pain began to spread from the tip of her tailbone, slowly escalating and coming in shorter intervals. Jiyoung soon found herself ripping off the corners of her hospital pillow and howling in pain. As the long labour continued, she felt like a Lego figure being twisted at an anatomically impossible angle and being separated at the waist, but her cervix wasn't dilated enough and there was no sign of the baby descending. As the contractions intensified, Jiyoung repeatedly said only one thing as if possessed: 'Epi ... epidural ... epidural ... please ... I beg of you ...' The epidural indeed allowed the couple two and a half hours of peace, but the pain after the brief respite was incomparably more intense than before.

Jiwon, a baby girl, was born at four in the morning. The baby was so sweet Jiyoung cried even more than she did during her labour. But Jiwon cried day and night until she was picked up, and Jiyoung had to do chores, go to the toilet and take naps while holding the infant. Breastfeeding every two hours and therefore unable to sleep for more than two hours at a time, she cleaned the house more thoroughly than before, washed the baby's clothes and fabrics, fed herself well so she would produce enough milk and cried far more than she'd ever cried in her life. Above all, she hurt all over.

She couldn't move her wrists at all. One Saturday morning, she left the baby with Daehyun and went to the nearby orthopaedist's clinic she'd visited when she hurt her ankle. The old man said her wrists were inflamed, but it wasn't serious. Was she in a line of work that was hard on the wrists? She said she gave birth not long ago.

'All your joints become weak after you give birth,' he

nodded as if to say, *That explains it.* 'I can't prescribe any-thing too strong if you're breastfeeding. Do you have time to come to physical therapy?'

Jiyoung shook her head.

'Try to rest your wrists. No other solution.'

'I can't,' Jiyoung sighed quietly. 'I have to look after the baby, do the washing and the cleaning ...'

The doctor chuckled to himself. 'Back in the day, women used clubs to do the laundry, lit fires to boil baby clothes, and crawled around to do the sweeping and mop-ping. Don't you have a washing machine for laundry and vacuum cleaner for cleaning? Women these days – what have you got to whine about?'

Dirty laundry doesn't march into the machine by itself, Jiyoung thought. *The clothes don't wash themselves with detergent and water, march back out when they're done and hang themselves on clotheslines. The vacuum doesn't roll around with a wet and dry rag, wipe the floor, and wash and dry the rags for you. Have you ever even operated a washing machine or a vacuum cleaner?*

The doctor checked Jiyoung's previous records, said he'd prescribe drugs that are safe for breastfeeding and clicked the computer mouse a few times. *Back in the day, physicians had to go through filing cabinets to find records and write notes and prescriptions by hand. Back in the day, office clerks had to run around the office with paper reports to track down their bosses for their approval. Back in the day, farmers planted by hand and harvested with sickles. What do these people have to whine about these days?* No one is insensitive enough to say that. Every field has its technological advances and evolves in the direction that reduces the amount of physical labour required, but people are particularly reluctant to admit that the same is true for domestic labour. Since she became a full-time housewife, she often noticed that there was a polarised attitude regarding domestic labour. Some demeaned it as 'bumming around at home', while others glorified it as 'work that sustains life', but none tried to calculate its monetary value. Probably because the moment you put a price on something, someone has to pay.

Jiyoung's mother couldn't help her recover from the pregnancy because she was busy with the porridge shop. Business was not what it used to be since a wider selection of restaurants moved into the commercial building, and reducing the number of workers to lessen costs meant the mother had to put in extra hours. Still, the shop brought in enough to support the younger brother, who was opting to prolong his education. The mother brought Jiyoung leftovers from the porridge shop whenever she could.

'I'm so proud of my skin-and-bones little girl. Having a baby of her own, breastfeeding, and raising it without my help. That's the almighty power of maternal love.'

'What was it like when you were raising us? Wasn't it tough? Didn't you regret having so many? Were you almighty, too?'

'Ugh. Don't even get me started. Your sister was loud from the very start. She cried so hard day and night that I was always running to the hospital to see if there was something wrong with her. I had three, your father never changed a single nappy, and your grandmother took three meals a day at home like clockwork. I had so much to do, I was falling asleep all the time, aches and pains all over – it was hell.'

Why didn't Jiyoung's mother ever speak up? No one had shared this in detail with Jiyoung – not her mother, relatives, older friends, or even friends her own age who'd had children. The babies on television or in movies were all pretty and cute, and mothers were always portrayed as beautiful and noble. Jiyoung was responsible and equal to the task of raising her child well, but she didn't want to hear people tell her how proud they were of her or how noble she was. These comments made her feel guilty about being exhausted.

The year Jiyoung married, a documentary on natural births aired on television. This was followed by multiple publications on the subject, and the sudden widespread popularity of natural births, the crux being minimal medical intervention and a natural birthing experience in which mother and baby make their own decisions. But delivery has to do with the safety of two lives. Jiyoung chose to give birth in a hospital with the help of experts because she had decided it was the safer way, and believed the birthing plan was a decision based on the parents' values and circumstances, not something to make a value judgement on. However, a significant number of media outlets reported on the possible adverse effects of medical treatment and medication on newborns – their causal relationship speculative – to arouse guilt and fear. People who pop a painkiller at the smallest hint of a migraine, or who need anaesthetic cream to remove a mole, demand that women giving birth should gladly endure the pain, exhaustion and mortal fear. As if that's maternal love. This idea of 'maternal love' is spreading like religious dogma. Accept Maternal Love as your Lord and Saviour, for the Kingdom is near!

'Thank you for bringing us food every time, Ma. I would have starved to death without you.'

Jiyoung only said 'thank you'. There was nothing else she could say to her mother after all this time.

Her former work colleague Kang Hyesu took a day

off and came for a visit bearing babygrows, nappies and lip gloss.

'Why the lip gloss?'

'I'm wearing it now, see? Nice colour, huh? You and I have similar skin tone, so I figured it'd look good on you, too.'

Jiyoung was happy that Hyesu didn't say things like, 'Mothers are women, too' or, 'Get out of those sweats and doll up every once in a while.' *I saw this and thought it'd look good on you.* The end. Clean and simple. Jiyoung felt better, and tried on the lip gloss. It really did look good on her, and that made her even happier.

They ordered Chinese and caught up on news and gossip. In between their conversation, Jiyoung breastfed Jiwon, fed her solid food, changed her nappy, walked around the house to comfort her when she cried and put her down for a nap. Hyesu was reluctant to handle Jiwon, saying she was afraid she'd hurt her, but warmed up the baby food in the microwave, fetched clean nappies and took care of the dishes.

'She's adorable and lovely,' said Hyesu, after watching Jiwon sleep for a long time. 'I'm not saying I want one, though.'

'She really is adorable and lovely,' Jiyoung agreed. 'But I'm not saying you should get one of these. I swear. But *if* you get one, I'll give you Jiwon's hand-me-downs.'

'What if it's a boy?'

'Do you know how much baby clothes cost? If you had a baby and someone offered you clothes for it, you wouldn't care if they were pink or crap-brown.'

Hyesu roared with laughter.

Jiyoung asked why Hyesu had taken a day off in the middle of peak season, and she said there'd been a scandal at the office. The ladies' room turned out to have a spycam hidden in the cubicles. The culprit was the building security agent in his twenties. Around two years ago, when the commercial building business association negotiated a deal with a new security firm, the old security guards on the ground floor were all replaced by young agents. Some said they felt safer with younger security agents around, while others said that the agents were scarier than burglars. Jiyoung had wondered what happened to the old security guards who were laid off.

The more disturbing part of this scandal was how people found out. It turned out that the security agent frequently uploaded the spycam pictures on a pornography site, of which a male section manager at Jiyoung's company had been a member. It didn't take long before the section manager recognised the ladies' room structure and the women's clothing, and realised the subjects in the pictures were actually his colleagues. But rather than reporting this to the police or victims, he shared these pictures with his male colleagues in the office. No one yet fully knows how many men passed the pictures around, what kind of conversations they had about them, how many photos, or for how long. But one of the male employees who saw the pictures urged a female employee (whom he was secretly dating) to use the ladies' room on a different floor. Feeling suspicious, this female employee pressed her boyfriend until he fessed up to the whole story. She couldn't report this to the authorities or the police, however, because they were keeping their relationship a secret. After agonising over what to do, she confided in her closest colleague, who happened to be Kang Hyesu.

'I notified every woman in the office. We searched for the cameras together and reported the case to the police,' said Hyesu. 'They are all getting investigated: the psycho security agent and the office perverts who passed the pictures around.'

'That's repulsive. Just repulsive.' Jiyoung didn't know what to say other than this. Then it occurred to her that her photo might have been taken, and this made her wonder, if so, who saw them and whether they were float-ing around on the internet right this minute. As though she knew what Jiyoung was thinking, Hyesu added that the spycams had been installed last summer after Jiyoung left the company.

'I'm seeing a therapist, actually,' said Hyesu. 'It's driving me crazy. Although I pretend I'm okay, laughing out loud around people, it feels like the whole world is recognising me from the pictures. Even random eye contact with strangers makes me wonder if that person has seen my pictures, and when someone smiles at me I think the person is mocking me. Most women in the office are on meds or getting therapy. Jungeun overdosed on sleeping pills and had to get her stomach pumped. Some people left: two women from General Affairs, Choi Hyeji and Park Seonyoung, the assistant section managers.'

Listening to Hyesu, Jiyoung thought how her picture would have been taken by one of the spycams if she hadn't quit. Shaken up just like other female employees at the company, she might have needed meds and eventually quit her job. She never suspected an ordinary person like herself could be a target of pornographic pictures floating around the web. The *security agent* set up hidden cameras in the women's toilets, and her *male colleagues* passed them around. Hyesu said she would never be able to trust a man again.

'The accused male employees blame us for being too harsh with them,' she added. 'They say they neither set up those cameras nor took the pictures, they just saw some photos posted on a website everyone has access to, and *we* are treating them like sexual offenders. They *distributed* the pictures and were complicit in the crimes, but they don't understand why that's wrong. It blows my mind.'

Hyesu explained that Eunsil, the team leader, along with several victims who chose to fight back, was coping with the situation by getting advice from a women's organisation. She was also preparing to leave the company and take some of the female staff with her to start her own business, because the male director of the company denied victims' demands that the company officially apologise to them, promise to take measures for prevention and punish those responsible. All he wanted was to quietly close this case: *It'll ruin this company's reputation if word gets around in the field. The accused male employees have families and parents to protect, too. Do you really want to destroy people's lives like this? Do you want people to find out that your pictures are out there?* These obviously self-serving words of absurdity flew out of the mouth of the director, who was considered to be progressive and sensible compared to his peers. It was the last straw for Eunsil.

'The fact that they have families and parents,' Eunsil retorted, 'is why they shouldn't do these things, not why we should forgive them. You should come to your senses yourself. Maybe you'll be lucky to save your ass this time,

KIM JIYOUNG, BORN 1982

but if you keep sweeping things under the carpet, you'll soon have another incident like this. You know this company hasn't done the mandatory staff seminars for sexual harassment, right?'

In fact, Eunsil was scared and exhausted herself. All of them – the team leader Eunsil, Kang Hyesu and the victims standing with them – wanted this case to be resolved soon so that they could go back to their lives. While offenders were in fear of losing a small part of their privilege, the victims were running the risk of losing everything.

Jung Jiwon started daycare a little past twelve months, and adjusted to the new environment surprisingly well. She was dropped off at 9.30 a.m., had a small snack, had playtime, had lunch, came back before 1 p.m., had a wash and took a nap. Not counting drop-off and pick-up time, Kim Jiyoung now had approximately three hours to herself. Most of that time was spent doing laundry and the dishes, tidying up, and making snacks and food for the baby. She hardly had a moment to sit down and enjoy a cup of coffee.

In fact, according to statistics, a stay-at-home mother with a baby under the age of two has four hours and ten minutes a day to herself, and a mother who sends her baby to daycare has four hours and twenty-five minutes, which makes only a fifteen-minute difference between those two groups. This means mothers can't rest even when they send their baby to daycare. The only difference is whether they do the housework with their baby beside them or without.[19] It was a huge load off for Jiyoung that she could have a moment to focus on getting chores done.

The daycare teacher said Jiwon was a good kid and was getting along well enough that she could try napping at daycare and going home a little later. Jiyoung said she'd pick her up right after lunch for now, but knowing she'd have more time to herself sparked an interest in starting something new.

Before Jiwon came along, the couple had saved up and paid off the loan on the deposit for the flat. But after the two-year lease ran out, the landlord raised the rent deposit by another 60 million won, which forced the couple to take out another loan. They couldn't afford to buy a place for a three-person family on Daehyun's income alone, and paying off a mortgage would become an even greater challenge once Jiwon started kinder-garten and after-school programmes. Jiyoung felt the pressure to bring in money. Housing, the cost of living,

19 'The End of Housewives,' *The Hankyoreh*, 21, V, 948.

the cost of education – all three were rising like the sky was the limit. Apart from those who'd inherited a lot or the select few high-income households, everyone was stretched thin.

Jiyoung knew many mothers who began working again as soon as they could send their children to daycare. Some freelanced in their given field instead of working full time; others went into the private education market by working as private tutors, cram-school teachers, or tutoring small groups out of their own homes. The most common scenario was getting a part-time job, such as a cashier, waitress, telemarketer or service worker, changing water purifier filters. According to reports, more than half of the women who quit their jobs are unable to find new work for more than five years. Even if they do manage to find new work, it is quite common for them to end up with jobs that are more menial than their previous employment. Compared to the jobs they had before childbirth, the ratio of women working in places with four or fewer employees doubles. Fewer women get manufacturing and office jobs, while a greater number end up in the hotel industry, restaurant business and sales. Frequently, the pay also decreases.[20]

---

20 Kim Yeongok, 'Status of Women with Career Break and Policy Tasks,' Analysis of 2015 Labor Market by Korea Employment Information Service.

Ever since government-funded childcare became available, young mothers have been censured for leaving their children at daycare to go for coffee, get their nails done and go shopping in department stores. The reality is that very few couples in their thirties are able to afford such a lifestyle. Far more mothers wait tables at restaurants and coffee shops, give other women manicures and work as sales assistants at department stores for the minimum wage. Since Jiwon was born, Jiyoung wondered each time she ran into working women her age: *Does she have a child? How many months old? Who's looking after it?* Many people don't want to accept the evident fact that all difficulties in life – stagnant economy, high cost of living, adverse labour environment and so on – affect both men and women equally.

Jiyoung had just dropped off her daughter at daycare and stopped by the supermarket to pick up some food when she saw a sign at the ice-cream store by the entrance. They were looking for weekday part-time workers: '10 to 4. 5600 won per hour. Housewives welcome.' That got Jiyoung's attention. The current part-timer also seemed like a housewife. She got herself a cup of ice cream and enquired about the part-time job. She explained amiably that she was also a mother of two who had worked there for four years while the children were at daycare. She said she was having to quit because her first child was starting first grade. She was very sorry to go.

'Work isn't very busy on weekdays because the store is inside the building, and there are even fewer customers once it gets cold. My arms were sore from scooping at first, but I got the hang of it.'

'Aren't you supposed to sign a contract and receive benefits after two years?'

'Oh, boy. You don't know anything about part-time work, do you? There are no part-time jobs where you sign a contract and get benefits. *Start work tomorrow. Yes, sir.* It's like that. You get a verbal agreement, start working, they pay you sometimes through your bank account, some-times through your husband's bank account. My employer was kind enough to offer me a small severance since I had worked here for a long time.'

Maybe it was because they were both mothers – or because Jiyoung didn't know anything about part-time work – that the ice-cream lady seemed to want to give her the job. She said there weren't many jobs that you could do while the kids were at daycare, that Jiyoung would not find anything much better than this and that she would take down the sign to give Jiyoung time to think about it and give her a call ASAP. Jiyoung said she'd discuss it with her husband, and was about to leave when the lady said, 'I have a college degree, too, you know.'

For some reason Jiyoung choked up at the lady's sudden confession. For the rest of that day, she couldn't stop thinking about what the lady had said. When Daehyun returned late from work that night, Jiyoung asked for his opinion. Daehyun was deep in thought, with his eyes fixed on the clock.

'Is this what you want to do?' he asked.

Frankly, Jiyoung didn't like ice cream. She wasn't interested in ice cream, nor did she see herself studying something related to it or pursuing a career in a related area. There was no prospect of going from part-timer to staff on contract, manager and a more desirable department in the ice-cream company. She would probably be on the minimum wage until the day she left. The job had no future, but the immediate benefits did come to mind: a 700,000-won monthly income was no small addition to an average-income home. The work didn't require that they get a sitter, and she could more or less balance work, childcare and housework. It was not an easy decision.

'Is this what you want to do?' he asked again and she said no.

'Of course, one can't go through life only doing what one wants to do. But, Jiyoung, I'm doing what I want to do. I can't advise you to do something you don't want to do when I made you quit the job you enjoyed while I continue to do what I want to do. Anyway, that's my two cents for now.'

Jiyoung found herself deliberating over her future career again for the first time in ten years. Whereas her priority a decade ago was her skills and interests, there were so many more variables to consider now. The most important thing was being able to look after Jiwon as much as possible – a job that allowed her to simply send Jiwon to daycare and not hire a sitter.

While working at the marketing agency, Jiyoung had always wanted to be a news reporter. Realistically, it would have been difficult for her to get hired as a reporter through recruitment tests, but a freelance reporter or contributor had seemed like an attainable goal. The possibility of starting something new made her heart flutter with long-forgotten excitement. First, she looked into schools teaching journalism, but most of the programmes only had evening classes aimed at full-time workers coming to school after work. Daycare centres would be closed by then, and even if her husband left work punctually, by the time she got to school the first half of the class would be over. She could opt to hire an evening babysitter, but it was difficult to find sitters who could work just at night for a short period of time. The fact that she had to hire a babysitter simply to take classes, not even to work, made her feel exhausted already. The cost of tuition, plus babysitting, was burdensome too.

Daytime programmes were mostly about hobbies or getting licences for teaching reading, writing or history to children. It felt like someone was saying, 'Have a hobby if you can afford it. If not, teach your children or others.' Her career potential and areas of interest were being limited just because she had a baby. A feeling of helplessness quickly replaced the excitement she had felt.

By the time she returned to the ice-cream store, they had already filled the position. Jiyoung swore that if she ever came across another part-time job that offered the hours and pay she wanted, she would take it regardless of what it was.

The heatwave abated, followed by real autumn days. Jiyoung picked up her daughter from daycare and put her in her pushchair. On the way to the nearby park to get some air and sun before it grew too cold, Jiwon fell asleep. Jiyoung thought about turning around and heading home, but kept going because it was nice out. A new coffee shop that had opened across the street from the park was offering discounts. Jiyoung got herself an Americano and sat on a park bench.

Jiwon was asleep with a long, clear drool hanging off the corner of her mouth, and Jiyoung enjoyed coffee in the park for the first time in a long while. On the next bench over was a group of office workers drinking coffee from the same café. They looked to be around Jiyoung's age. Knowing how tired, frustrated and exhausted they must be, she still couldn't help looking at them enviously. One of the guys on the bench glanced over at Jiyoung and whispered something to his colleagues. Jiyoung couldn't make out every word, but she could hear bits and pieces of their conversation: *I wish I could live off my husband's paycheque ... bum around and get coffee ... mum-roaches got it real cushy ... no way I'm marrying a Korean woman ...*

Jiyoung rushed out of the park, spilling hot coffee on the back of her hand. Jiwon woke up and began to cry, but Jiyoung didn't notice as she ran home, pushing the buggy ahead of her. She was in a daze all afternoon. She fed Jiwon cold soup, forgot the nappy and had to change Jiwon out of her soiled clothes; she also forgot that she had done a load of laundry and hung the wrinkled clothes to dry after Jiwon went to bed. When Daehyun returned from a business dinner after midnight with a bag of red-bean-filled goldfish cakes, she realised she hadn't had lunch or dinner. When she told him that she hadn't eaten all day, he asked if something was wrong.

'People call me "mum-roach".'

Daehyun heaved a long sigh and said, 'Those online

comments are written by dumb pre-teens. No one actually uses that word in real life. No one thinks that about you.'

'No, I heard it with my own ears today. At the park across the street, some office guys, thirty-ish, wearing suits. They called me that.'

Jiyoung told him what happened that day. She'd felt shocked and mortified at the time, and she had wanted to get away that instant. But recounting the situation made her flush, and her hands shook.

'The coffee was 1500 won. They were drinking the same coffee, so they must have known how much it was. Tell me – don't I deserve to drink a 1500-won cup of coffee? I don't care if it's 1500 won or 15 million won. It's nobody's business what I do with the money my husband made. Am I stealing from you? I suffered deathly pain having our child. My routine, my career, my dreams, my entire life, my self – I gave it all up to raise our child. And I've become vermin. What do I do now?'

Daehyun gently drew her towards him and embraced her by the shoulders. Not knowing what to say, he patted her on the back and repeated, 'That's not true. Don't think like that.'

Jiyoung became different people from time to time. Some of them were living, others were dead, all of them women she knew. No matter how you looked at it, it wasn't a joke or a prank. Truly, flawlessly, completely, she became that person.

2016

This is my rough summary of Kim Jiyoung's life so far, based on Jiyoung and her husband Jung Daehyun's accounts. The patient comes in for 45-minute sessions twice a week, and while her symptoms have decreased in frequency, they have yet to disappear. In order to alleviate her depression and insomnia, I have prescribed her a set of antidepressants and sleeping pills.

I suspected dissociative disorder (which I had only previously encountered through case studies) when I first heard Daehyun's description of Jiyoung's symptoms, but I concluded, based on my initial session with Jiyoung, that she had a typical case of postnatal depression that progressed to childcare depression. However, as the treatment continued, my conviction in this diagnosis started to fade. That isn't to say that she is guarded or antagonistic. She does not complain about the suffering and injustice of her current reality, nor does she keep revisiting childhood traumas. She doesn't open up without encouragement, but once she gets going, she unearths long-buried memories on her own and describes them articulately in a calm, logical manner. Looking at the moments and scenes in Kim Jiyoung's life that she chose to share in our sessions, I realise that I may have diagnosed her hastily. I'm not saying I was wrong, only that I've come to realise there is a world that I wasn't aware of.

If I were an average male in his forties, I would have gone through my entire life without this awareness. Only by following the medical career of my wife (she was a better student than I when we were in medical school together) who made compromise after compromise – from going after a tenure position as a professor of ophthalmology, to contract doctor, to giving up on her career entirely – was I enlightened as to what it means to live as a woman, especially as a mother, in Korea. Frankly, it's only natural that men remain unaware unless they encounter special circumstances as I have, because men are not the main players in childbirth and childcare.

The in-laws living far south and her own parents living in the States, my wife made it through each day, one day at a time, with the help of a revolving door of nannies to look after our son. When he finally started school, she enrolled him in an after-school programme and then a dojo. His taekwondo master picked him up from school and took him to the dojo where the boy practised taekwondo and skip rope while waiting for his mum to finish work. My wife said she felt she finally had time to breathe. But it wasn't even summer vacation before she got called into school – the boy stuck a pencil in the back of his class-mate's hand.

He apparently walked around during class. He spat in his own soup and then ate it. He kicked the other children in the shin and cursed at the teachers. My wife was shocked. He had sometimes cried when he didn't want to go to daycare, when he didn't want Mummy to go to work, but everyone had thought of him as a well-mannered, good boy. The teacher suspected ADHD, and I disagreed, but she wouldn't listen to me.

'I'm a psychiatric specialist. You'd rather believe the teacher?'

Seething in silence for a moment, my wife glared at me and said, 'You see the patient, look them in the eye and listen to them to get a diagnosis. You spend maybe ten minutes a day with the boy? And you're glued to your phone the entire ten minutes you're sitting with him! How could you possibly know? You can tell by watching him sleep? Listening to his breathing? You possessed? You a psychic, not a psychiatrist?'

In my defence, I was very busy around that time because my practice had relocated and expanded. I had emails and messages I had to keep tabs on using my phone, and I sometimes checked the news while I had the phone out, but I swear I never played games or chatted on the phone. Anyway, everything she said was true, so I had nothing to say. I didn't see the connection between my wife working and the boy being distracted, but the teacher prescribed 'stay-at-home mummy' at least for the first half of elementary school, and my wife took a break from work. She got up even earlier than she did for work to make our son's breakfast, wake him up and wash him herself, feed and clothe him, drop him off at school, pick him up from school, and have art and piano tutors come by for lessons. At night, she slept with the boy in his room. She said she'd return to work when he got better, and that she'd had a talk with a senior colleague and arranged a position for when she was ready to go back. She called up that colleague not long thereafter to cancel. He's not showing improvement, she said.

The last day of that year, I came home late after an end-of-year get-together with high-school friends. My wife was still up, sitting at the kitchen table hard at work writing something. She was solving maths problems. Cute illustrations and pictures in a palette of primary colours took up more than half the pages of the elementary-school maths workbook.

'Why are you doing his homework?'

'He's on vacation, and elementary schools these days don't make kids solve workbooks over vacation. Not that you'll know.'

'Then what's that?'

'Just for fun. Maths these days is different from what we learned in school. It's really difficult and really fun. Look at this. This is the real Seoul City Public Bus numbering system. The goal is to guess the bus number by looking at the chart, map and bus schedule. Isn't this interesting?'

I didn't think it was interesting enough to stay up that late for, but I said sure, and went to bed because I was sleepy and I didn't want to get into it.

That weekend, I found more maths workbooks in the recycling. My wife had gone through all of them. All this time, I had thrown out volumes of maths workbooks thinking our son was really into the subject. I could have just thought of the workbooks as her cute, odd hobby, but it got on my nerves. She'd been a maths prodigy: she'd won maths competitions and Olympiads all through school, got 100 per cent on all twelve mid-term and final maths exams over three years of high school, and missed one question on the maths section of the college entrance exam. I couldn't understand why someone like her was so into elementary-school maths workbooks. When I asked, she said offhandedly, 'It's fun.'

'For someone your level? It's literally kids' stuff.'

'No, it's fun. It's really fun. 'Cause this is the one thing I can control these days.'

My wife is still doing the maths workbooks, and I wish she'd do something more interesting. Something she's good at, that she likes, that she really wants to do, not something she does because there's nothing else. I wish the same for Kim Jiyoung.

I look at the small family photo on my desk. It's from our son's first birthday party. He looks so little and almost unrecognisable, whereas my wife and I look exactly the same. When it occurs to me that we have not taken a single family photo since, I feel a pang of guilt. At that moment, someone knocks on my office door. Someone must not have left for the day yet.

Lee Suyeon, one of our counsellors, gingerly walks into the room, places a small cactus on the windowsill, and then offers the usual words of farewell: 'Thank you for everything. I'm sorry I have to quit. I hope I get to work with you again in the future.' I reply with similarly per-functory words: 'It's too bad. Thank you for all your help.

We would love to have you back again.' Today is her last day. Considering the doctor put her on bed rest, I wonder why she's here until this hour.

'I was just organising the referral files,' she explains without prompting, seeing the perplexed look on my face.

The clinic director recommended Suyeon a year ago and she has been working with us since then. After six years of marriage and years of trying, she finally got pregnant but was warned her condition was unstable. After a few miscarriage scares, she decided to 'temporarily' give up her job. I was displeased by the news at first, wondering why she couldn't just take a couple of months off instead of quitting altogether, but I guess this is for the best since she'll be going on maternity leave soon anyway, and then causing inconveniences at the clinic by taking sick days for herself, for her child, etc.

Suyeon has undoubtedly been a great employee. She has pretty – some would say elegant – features, a neat and snappy way of dressing, and a quick wit and charm. She even remembers how I take my coffee – which coffee shop, how many shots of espresso – and brings it in on the way to work. Cheerful and warm, she has a smile on her face for co-workers and patients alike. Unfortunately, because of her suddenly leaving, more patients have decided to terminate therapy rather than be referred to another counsellor at our clinic. That's a bottom-line loss for the clinic. Even the best female employees can cause many problems if they don't have the childcare issue taken care of. I'll have to make sure her replacement is unmarried.